A PLAGUED SEA

A PLAGUED SEA

KIM BO-YOUNG

TRANSLATED BY SOPHIE BOWMAN

TOR PUBLISHING GROUP
NEW YORK

This is a work of fiction. All of the names, characters, organizations, places, and events portrayed in this work are either products of the author's imagination or used fictitiously.

A PLAGUED SEA

Originally published in South Korea as 역병의 바다 (Yeokbyeongui bada) by Alma (알마).

A Nightfire Book
Published by Tom Doherty Associates / Tor Publishing Group
120 Broadway
New York, NY 10271

www.torpublishinggroup.com

Nightfire™ is a trademark of Macmillan Publishing Group, LLC.

EU Representative: Macmillan Publishers Ireland Ltd, 1st Floor, The Liffey Trust Centre,117–126 Sheriff Street Upper, Dublin 1, D01 YC43

The Library of Congress Cataloging-in-Publication Data is available upon request.

ISBN 978-1-250-38075-3 (hardcover)
ISBN 978-1-250-38076-0 (ebook)

First U.S. Edition: 2026

Printed in the United States of America

10 9 8 7 6 5 4 3 2 1

Dedication TK

A PLAGUED SEA

Your Excellency the President,
[REDACTED]

I have no way of knowing whether this letter will really reach Your Excellency, but if there is anyone at all who will take an interest in what I witnessed that day in that village, I will not tire, and keep writing as long as I am able.

Even now, if I only think of the night that followed that day, it is as though a rake-like hand is squeezing my heart, my blood dries in place, and I have to fight for my next breath. It is as if the mouth of hell opens wide to devour me, chomping on my body. Every night in my dreams I return to that fishing village. All night long I am chased through pitch-dark alleyways reeking with the briny stench of fish by ghastly monsters I wish I could forget. Then my own gruesome cries startle me awake.

I greet each morning with despair, knowing that I have grown weaker than I was the day before. I do not know how much longer I will live. But until the truth of that day is brought to light, I cannot stop . . .

Yours Humbly,
Ha Woojin

PhD in Biochemistry, ████ University
Researcher, Korea Contagious Diseases Society
Budget Consultant, National Treasury Support Initiative for East Sea Disease Sufferers
Director, Association of Intellectuals for Protecting Humankind from Ancient Species

---

PROLOGUE

In the early hours of the morning, the waiting room at Cheongnyangni Station doesn't belong to passengers. It's pretty much a bunkhouse for the homeless. The lined-up rows of benches facing the ticket gates are packed tight with them.

All bundled up in layers and layers of clothing, they lie, not even their breath making a sound. One, unidentifiable as male or female, is sitting like a roly-poly doll, their face wrapped up in a scarf and wooly hat, cocooned in a quilt with a layer of plastic on top of it that they have somehow fixed in place with tape. It's clear that they are determined not to expose a single inch of their skin to this harsh world. They may look as though they have their gaze on the TV, but nothing is registering in those eyes.

As the eastern sky starts to show dusky light, passengers arrive, one by one, and form a throng, and the homeless people hide themselves, as though scrubbed away by an eraser. Older-middle-aged women gather together laughing, wearing bright red and pink padded jackets and hats with floral patterns, dragging colorful striped travel cases.

The faithful evangelists have shown up to work again today, taking their places outside the station. Setting up their signboards, crammed with bold letters in red that say things like, "Check the back of your family and friends' necks for 666, the sign of the devil," "When the day of judgment comes 144,000 people will receive a summons to ascend." They lug out the loudspeakers and boomboxes they've been using since who knows when, and as they take their seats in their usual spot, they warmly greet the street vendor who is just packing up and going home after a long night selling liquor and snacks to eat with it. The small-time prophets have rubbed off and rewritten the date of judgment day so many times that the wood on that spot on the signboard is all worn down.

I'd had my attention on the woman sitting on the bench opposite for a while, even though it's rude to stare at a stranger.

She had a richness to her skin, so I wondered whether one of her parents might have been Vietnamese, or from somewhere else in Southeast Asia. She looked to be in her midthirties, and had a beautiful face. But all the hairs on her body were standing on end, and she was shrunk into herself, as though a passing ant might attack her. The man beside her—who looked to be twenty years her senior and wore his unmistakable ill temper on his face—took up three seats, his thighs spread out as far as they would reach. The contrast made me bristle.

"Auntie! Auntie! Look at this fish, it's so funny looking," Hyun said, standing between my legs and shaking my smartphone in my face.

For a while after we got here, sleepy in the early morning, she had been throwing herself on the waiting room floor and rolling around, stretching out and shuffling like a snail. She only calmed down when I gave her my phone to watch YouTube.

It must have been some kind of documentary on the deep sea. An anglerfish was swimming through black water where white organic matter was falling like snow. The anglerfish's eyes bulged, and needle-sharp teeth stuck out in all directions from its mouth.

Its body looked squishy like a balloon, and there were nubby protruding bumps all over its skin. And there was a tiny male anglerfish, dangling from its tummy, sucking nutrients from its mate. About half of the male's head was already melted, absorbed into her.

"Why are they so ugly like that?" Hyun asked, tapping the screen with a glitter-painted fingernail.

"The deep sea is veeery deep, so they can't see anything down there. And because no one can see anything down there, they can't see what anyone looks like . . . so there's no need to be pretty."

It was nothing to laugh at, but my tone of voice and my gestures made Hyun burst into a bubbling giggle.

"That sounds great," Hyun said, sighing as I took back my phone.

"What's great about that?"

Hyun didn't reply and lay down again, rubbing her pink dress covered in lace and dangling ribbons into the floor. She wore a red headband with a big bow on it, and her shoulder-length hair had been permed straight and dip-dyed pink at the ends. She'd been at the hairdresser for hours the day before, because she had to look pretty in the pictures of our trip.

I crouched down and nuzzled Hyun's cheek. "Your mom and dad will come back from their business trip and join us tomorrow by train."

"Tell them not to come. I want to play, just you and me."

"So you expect *me* to shell out for all the accommodation and meals?"

"What does shell out mean?"

A high-pitched *ka-tok* sounded from my pocket. When I opened Kakao Talk on my phone there was a whole string of messages from my older sister.

Put on an English-language YouTube video for her at 10am. Remind her she'll get one smack for every question she gets wrong on the test.

Don't feed her anything from a street stall. Our baby has a sensitive enough stomach as it is, she can't go catching parasites.

And don't forget to register with Sarang Hospital as soon as you get there. You know my husband's friend from high school is the director. You'll have to contact them when the kid gets an upset stomach or something from the water.

Oh, and at two o'clock . . .

Ka-tok! The sound made me jump, and I rushed to turn off notifications.

"What did mom say? I bet she's talking crazy again."

". . . you shouldn't say that kind of thing about your mom."

"I wish she wouldn't come," Hyun whined.

She put her arms around my waist from the side and hugged tight. I patted her back.

"It might not be easy, but do your best to put up with her until you're grown up."

"And then what?"

"Um . . . you can tell your parents you're going to start a business, take their money, and then squander all of it! Or you could get your inheritance early and run off to a foreign country, take your auntie along as a bodyguard and pay me a salary—"

"What does squander mean?"

Just then the woman who had been on the bench opposite hurried back to her seat, plastic bags hanging from each arm.

One by one she unpacked bundles from one of the food stands, odeng and gimbap. It seemed her husband didn't approve of the food she had brought for him. It was written all over his face: he's exhausted, in a bad mood today, and truly believes it's all because his wife is shaping the entire world to spite him.

Smiling all the while, the woman picked up a piece of gimbap with chopsticks and was about to put it in the man's mouth when, with a *pok*, his fist struck her temple.

I bolted to my feet. The holiday-makers in colorful outfits turned around in shock. As if to say, "Oops, must've forgotten that we're out in public," the man spat on the ground and feigned indifference. It was as though he believed that if he erased his own thought, it would be wiped out of everyone else's minds too.

Clutching at the side of her head as it began to swell and redden, the woman looked around to gauge the reactions of the spectators, and gave an awkward laugh. From what I could see, the embarrassment of people watching him hit her was more troubling to her than the fact of getting hit. And she gave the man a reproachful look that said, "Darling you mustn't do such private things when everyone can see." If what had just taken place wasn't fresh in my memory, I could have mistakenly assumed they'd just kissed.

Perhaps because the eyes all around made her uncomfortable, the woman bowed her head low and headed to the bathrooms. I left Hyun where she was and followed her. I thought to myself, *What am I doing?* The woman is doing her best. She will have tried everything. There's nothing a random stranger could think of that she hasn't already considered.

I caught up with the woman at the end of the line that stretched out like a lizard's tail from the door to the women's bathroom. The woman turned back to look at me startled, like someone who has just been caught committing a crime.

"Uh, Hi."

I'm done for, done for, I thought. All that's left is for me to be cursed out. Who are you? Who do you think you are to interfere? Don't get involved in other people's business. What a joke you are!

"Well, uh, you see, I work for a security company." I took a business card out of my wallet and put it in the woman's hand. "If you need our services, just get in touch. Our company has lawyers and counselors, and connections with lots of other companies and experts. You could even just call for a chat, if you want."

The woman stood there looking down at the business card. She didn't lash out or start hurling insults. Instead, she inspected me from head to toe. "You're a bodyguard?"

Her accent was flawless. Perhaps she was second generation, because she didn't seem foreign at all.

"I competed in the National Sports Festival when I was young. And I was an amateur athlete for a while . . ."

"My husband is a fisherman," the woman said, perhaps thinking we were exchanging introductions.

I just about managed to stop myself from going on, "Oh, I studied for a while to get a small-boat sailing license when I was a kid . . ." and letting the conversation descend into triviality. I hurried to leave before the woman found reason to chastise me. Well, you never know. This could be an opportunity. She might decide to contact someone, even if it's not our company. Maybe the local police. You can never predict what a person might do.

When I got back to the benches and was about to sit down, for some reason something felt off. Even more people than usual seemed to be making phone calls. Their faces were icy, and they spoke with urgency. Station employees came out of the office and walked around. They looked rushed, and their expressions were grave.

"Auntie, you keep getting calls."

Hyun rooted around in my jacket and took out my phone. When I looked at it, it wasn't a call but a disaster alert.

That was when the TV screen changed. The slapping waves of the East Sea replaced the morning talk show, and news flash subtitles raced across the bottom of the screen.

6.2 MAGNITUDE EARTHQUAKE 10KM OFF THE EAST COAST AT HAEWON PORT . . . UNPRECEDENTED—RESIDENTS URGED TO EVACUATE—AFTERSHOCKS EXPECTED—WATER TEMPERATURE RAPIDLY RISING—POSSIBLE UNDERWATER VOLCANIC ERUPTION—ALL BOATS TO RETURN TO PORT.

"That's where we're going today!" Hyun shouted, pointing at the screen.

And at the very same time the boarding announcement for the train to Gangneung flashed up on the departures board. Although they were murmuring to each other, people headed toward the ticket barriers as if by inertia. There were no specific warnings, and no one tried to stop them. It was probably just that there hadn't been time yet to work out what action to take.

"Hurry, Auntie, let's hurry." Hyun tugged at my leg. "If we don't, and they shut down the line, we'll be stuck here. Let's hurry."

It's inevitable that thoughts move slowly when we're confronted with unforeseen events. As though being pulled by a magnet, I chased after Hyun who was skipping along.

Hey, you've got to wait, I thought, following behind her with short quick steps, carrying the two massive suitcases that my sister and her husband had crammed with all sorts of stuff.

Later on, I would often recall that moment. I'd tell myself that if I'd caught up with Hyun, I could have persuaded her. "Listen Hyun . . . it seems like something's happened. Let's wait for a bit and take the next train." But as though Hyun knew I'd try to stop her, she slipped ahead every time I got near her.

The platform was peaceful. The train was waiting obediently in its place, and the stewards greeted passengers by the doors as though nothing was wrong.

"I hope there's another earthquake. So there's no way to get back."

Climbing up into the train, Hyun waved at me to hurry on.

"Then I'd never have to go home. I could just live with you, Auntie! Just the two of us."

1

THREE YEARS LATER

There were traces of the door having been opened.

The sand was pushed to one side. The wooden door was warped and there was mold and fungi growing from every crevice. Every time the sea wind hit the door it creaked a sorrowful cry. When I tried to open it, I found it locked from the inside.

The stupid jerk. If he was going to pretend not to be inside, he should have left it unlocked.

I rested my shoulder against the door to reduce the kickback and then shoved it hard.

With a crash, the screws holding the rusty hinges on were forced out and the door burst open. Clouds of dust billowed up from the floor like snow. The blustery wind swept ruthlessly through the house.

It was empty, with just a few things that no one wanted left lying around. Broken plates and plastic boxes, a toilet without a seat. The door to the bathroom had been pulled off, and there were holes in the wall where a washbasin and kitchen sink would have been. Cool moonlight seeped in through a window that was patched up with wood and nails, with an added glow from the lighthouse beam pulsing now and then. Some squatters made homeless by the flood must have boarded it up because there was nothing else to replace the broken glass. Just another abandoned house, clinging to the mountainside like the rest of Haewon Village.

The eastern sky had a dusky light in it, but the day was still early. I was intent on finishing up before dawn.

I placed my hand on the military knife that hung from the right-hand side of my belt. The knife fit snug in my palm . . . *today might be the day.* With all the restraint I could muster, I released the knife and clasped a baton in each hand.

As I stepped farther inside, I held the baton in my left hand up firmly to my face for defense and softly swung the other to intimidate. A musty salt smell stung my nose, different from the tang of human bodies. The salt smell of blood is metallic, from ferrous ion. What was stinging my nose now was the salty stench of rotting fish.

Sergeant Hyunjun had once informed me, as he leafed through a report, "That fishy smell comes from a compound called trimethylamine that helps fish regulate osmotic pressure. There's actually a genetic disorder called trimethylaminuria, where sufferers create and excrete excessive trimethylamine. It makes them stink of fish. The East Sea Disease has that same symptom."

If East Sea Disease only caused this stench, that would be great. But . . .

Some huge creature moved nimbly in the darkness. The movement wasn't right for a human, and the shape was too big for it to be a dog or cat. I twisted to block my opponent from the door. I'd checked before I entered: there was no other way in or out of the house.

"There'll be no time while we're fighting, so I'll say this in advance. You can request a lawyer and you have the right to remain silent."

Keeping the door in mind, I took a few more steps inside and tapped at the window with my baton. Softened by the humidity, the wood nailed across the window frame shook like paper.

"But as you already know, lawyers don't come to this village.

Better not to rely on one. And it'd be best if you don't exercise your right to remain silent, since it's a waste of time. You've already violated self-isolation thirteen times, and I'm close to losing my temper."

When I was done with my speech, I bashed the wood at the window with all my might.

As the planks splintered, the sweeping lighthouse beam streamed in, blinding. There was a bloodcurdling scream. The thing that made it ran at me covering its eyes.

I took off my jacket and threw it over his face. I was going to pull the sleeves across his neck to choke him, but with no hair on that slippery head, it slid right off.

As I staggered for footing, my opponent pounced on me, shrieking. I lost my balance and fell backward. I guarded my face with my left baton and grabbed his grasping arm with my right hand.

That bloodcurdling sound rang again in my ears. My opponent's arm was too long for his body. His bones had developed abnormally, making his elbows stick out. Veins showed through the skin pulled tight over his muscles, and his joints were a deep bruised blue. His fingers were unnaturally long, and there were blisters all along them and across the back of his hand. But even that arm wasn't so strange compared to this guy's face.

There were two or three extra teeth sticking out of his mouth, jamming the rest out of alignment. His lips curled away from them and his jawbone jutted out. Since his mouth couldn't close, drool dribbled down his chin and a foul stench rode his breath. His cheekbones protruded, and his face was swollen. The skin, pulled taut across his nose, made it look like only a set of nostrils. His bulging eyes were a deep, bloodshot red.

"Ph'ulu pulu fhtapa . . ." The diseased man tried to speak but it was hard to understand the gurgle from his ruined oral cavity.

This I could understand: A life sunk deep in terrible misfortune, and a heart that howled, hoping that the stifling pain inside might be eased a little by someone, anyone else, becoming as unfortunate as himself.

I'd heard that just three years ago this young man had been well known in the village for his good looks. I heard he had studied physical education at Hanzhong University, and was the pride of his family. People even said that once, when he had gone to Seoul with some friends, he'd been stopped in the street and given a business card by someone from a modeling agency. After catching East Sea Disease, skeletal abnormalities and facial deformities put an end to his looks. But just like so many of the infected, it was his mind that had suffered the most destruction.

Making a screeching wail, the monster grabbed my arms and forced them down. The baton descended bit by bit and pressed down hard into my throat.

"This . . . is your last . . . warning. You're interfering with a public official's duties . . . and you ignored your isolation order."

As I finished speaking, I swung my knee into the monster's crotch with all my might. The fact that they don't print how vulnerable that dangling organ is on the first page of first-year elementary school textbooks speaks volumes about how this world is tailored for the comfort of men.

As the monster collapsed wailing, I struck him hard with my baton. His nose shattered with a *pak*. The monster rolled on the floor, clutching his crotch and his face.

Gasping, I got up. Again, my hand found the military knife at my belt. *Today might just be the day.*

This jerk can't be locked up or put to death. The village's maritime police station was shut down, and there's no detention facility in the substation, which was the only judicial authority left. And the people in this village can't leave. Since we're all infected or carriers, we can't be locked up in any prison or brought to trial. The only punishment this village has is house arrest, whether for a petty thief or an armed robber. We lock them up at home, just like the infected people who would spread the disease. And there's no one to enforce all the house arrest orders. The only way to make sure someone in isolation doesn't leave the house was voluntary surveillance by villagers and the cooperation of their family. It's a miracle this damned situation has kept going for three years.

. . . today might just be the day.

Is there any reason to hold out any longer? Is there any reason left for me to stick to the straight and narrow in this isolated, abandoned village? When the administration and judicial systems have given up on us? In any case, I'll take a bad hit one day, in a fight like this, and bleed out in some secluded alleyway, or else be murdered by one of the infected with a grudge. What was I pushing so hard to defend?

Even if I left this jerk tied up in his house today, he'd be out again by tomorrow, spreading his germs all over the place. If he died here today, wouldn't some well-behaved child who hadn't yet been infected get to live a little longer?

My mind was half made up to pull my knife. But I held back and swung my batons.

2

I made it out of the house. On top of the rotting fish smell, I had to breathe in the stink of shit and piss as I tied the jerk's hands and feet, so when I was done, I felt like my head would crack open. I took out the carton of vinegar I kept in my pocket and sprayed some on myself. After sweaty fights with jerks like that, there was nothing I could really do about the smell, but this had become something like a ritual, something to calm my mind.

The sky was brightening from across the sea. The horizon burned with scarlet, and there was still a fingernail moon hung at the highest point of the indigo sky. Even in this utterly rotten time, this one view out from the slopes of the mountain was arrestingly beautiful.

Haewon Village is a neighborhood of about one hundred houses, packed like matchsticks on the slopes of a low mountain beneath a small lighthouse. Most of the houses are single story with blue-tiled roofs. The roofs received the blue darkness of the western sky and the scarlet of the east at once, and twinkled with an inky blue. The only roads into the village were Sunrise Road, which follows the East Sea coastline, and Dawn Road, which goes to the lighthouse. It's been three years since the two roads were blocked off. In that time the neglected asphalt cracked and split, and sinkholes appeared. Weeds grew where the surface collapsed, and soon the roads were no longer passable by car. The cars left behind by tourists who came to the village three years ago and got stuck here sit discarded, their windows smashed, mugwort and cockleburs growing all over them.

The streets were as quiet as a lake. Not one person caught my eye. Half the people in the village were critical patients with orders to isolate, and the rest were family members who cared for them. The fishing boats anchored in Haewon Port had been abandoned too and were now choked in by waterweeds.

I glared at the cursed island towering across the water. The rocky outcrop that appeared that day, three years ago.

The night of the earthquake, magma broke through the seabed and burst out from kilometers beneath the ocean floor. The volcano made a new island just off the shore from Haewon Port. Along the coast in both directions, to Daejin Port and Cheongok Port and all the way to Donghae City, the seabed rose five inches or so. A tidal wave flooded the coast and half of the homes in Haewon Village.

That wasn't the end of the disaster. The craggy island that burst up and the newly shallowed waters changed the flow of the current, and the sea around Haewon Port became a stagnant lake. In no time the coastal waters were overrun with plankton, and congealed into a sticky, viscous swamp. Masses of fish suffocated and died in the gluey water, and as their dead bodies washed up on shore and rotted, the stench hung in the village. The sailing routes were blocked, and within a few months all of the fish farms and the fish market closed down.

Along with the stench, a terrible virus spread. The symptoms were skin disease and skeletal deformity, accompanied by a foul smell. Spots and hives appeared on the skin of the infected, until it eventually became solid like wood. As their sweat glands closed up, sufferers' hair fell out, and the rising pressure in their eyes made them bulge. Most people think the disease rose from deep underground as the volcano surfaced long-buried geological strata, or that an ancient virus unknown to modern civilization hitched a ride on the parasites rampant in the putrefying water.

It's presumed that transmission occurs through prolonged contact, but nothing has been proven. Since there are lots of instances where the infection doesn't spread to other family members within a household, it's assumed that some people have antibodies, but all attempts to identify these antibodies have failed.

We were promised that the quarantine would end as soon as a vaccine was developed, but the virus didn't spread outside of the Donghae region, and as it became clear that the most serious symptoms of skeletal deformity only occurred within this village, the administration changed direction, merely tightening the lockdown. Almost every day the media churned out articles accusing Haewon of some inhumane act or another that could rationalize this punishment.

My phone rang. I put a cigarette in my mouth and pulled the phone from my pocket. The screen had cracked a long time ago. Only after pressing the power button a few times and shaking it did a splintered picture show up in distorted colors.

The police substation commander Jeon Sucheol's face filled the screen. Since the first year after the disaster, Commander Jeon had been living shut up inside his home. I'd heard he even made his wife, who has gallbladder cancer, go out to buy their necessities. There was also a rumor that he's stockpiled guns and bullets in his home and spends every day polishing them. He said that the local criminals bear such terrible resentment toward him that he can't come out. But really, what's he done for them to be resentful about? Once in a while he laments for over an hour about how public order would collapse if he, the commander of operations, fell sick. So even if he wanted to, he couldn't jeopardize the village by coming out. At those times all I can think is, whatever, no one cares, there's no need to maintain some pretense of concern and responsibility.

"What happened?"

I blew a long puff of smoke into the screen and replied, "He's dead."

Commander Jeon was taken aback. "That's your way of saying you caught him, right?"

"I said he's dead."

The commander disappeared from the screen and then came back. "Now hang on. You, you can't really mean you killed him? Think carefully. You don't mean it. Did you really kill him? What were you thinking? How am I supposed to face K-Kim Sunja now?"

"I broke his nose and some ribs. Left him pretty much dead. If you don't send someone there and get him to a hospital right away, he probably will die. Your call!"

I hung up and started walking. I hadn't gotten more than a few steps when I got a Kakao video call from Sergeant Hyunjun.

He looked as though I'd put him in an awkward position. Sergeant Hyunjun's case of East Sea Disease was only mild, but he had visible symptoms. His eyes protruded and black spots dotted his face. He'd grown two extra wisdom teeth, so his incisors stuck out too. But still, aside from vigilantes like me, this young guy was all the village had left in terms of law enforcement. He had gone out on patrol from early morning to late at night every single day for the last three years, monitoring both the severely ill and the law-breakers isolated in their homes. Right now, he was probably in his one-room home, preparing a pack of instant ramen and getting ready to head out to work.

"It sounds like you really went for it again?"

"That punk attacked me first."

"You know, don't you, that there are only fifteen general hospitals in the whole of Gangwon Province?" The extra vowels of his local accent were coming out. "And Sarang's the only one that accepts patients with East Sea Disease. They don't have an emergency room. If someone leaves our village hurt, they just die."

"Then it's the medical infrastructure that finished him, not me."

The sergeant heaved a deep sigh.

"I'll take care of the paperwork. Thankfully we haven't received any accusations or lawsuits so far, but . . . if it becomes an issue later on, I'll say that you did it under my orders."

"There's no need . . ."

"We can't pay you properly, or guarantee the safety of your work environment. The least I can do is take responsibility."

The sergeant disappeared from the screen. I pocketed my phone and trudged toward the seashore.

The color of the village changes halfway down the mountain. That's the line to which the tidal wave rose when it swallowed the village that day. The houses lower down are all brined in seawater and have dried seaweed on the roofs. Many were abandoned. Among the occasional houses that have been put in order most are fortune tellers or counseling offices. There are countless fortune tellers in this tiny village. It seems as though everyone here who ever read *The Book of Changes* or a fortune telling manual one time has opened up shop. The only methods left for imagining hope are readings of people's Four Pillars of Destiny and looking up their date of birth in the *Tojeong Bigyeol*.

The murals that had been painted to create a low-budget tourist attraction are ruined from the middle of the village down. The paint is blistered and peeling away, so that pretty children and fairies look like hideous monsters. Among them there are places where someone has come along and painted over them, defacing the figures to look like monsters and goblins.

I got another Kakao alert. It was Sergeant Hyunjun again, this time a text.

I'm telling you this just in case, but it would be better if you stayed home today, take it easy.

Sergeant Hyunjun's regional accent disappeared in writing.

Is there something going on?

No, there's nothing going on. What I'm saying is, there's too much nothing going on. Usually something happens once or twice a day. One person tries to escape, and one causes a disturbance, and one attempts suicide. And usually someone throws ramen soup dregs or an egg at me. But right now, the troublemakers are all so quiet they could be dead.

Is Professor Shim scheming something?

Before all this, Shim Yeongho was a professor of social welfare at Hanzhong University. He developed symptoms on the very first day of the disaster and went straight into self-isolation. From there he made a community for people infected with the East Sea Disease, and they communicated via Kakao Talk group chats and Daum message boards, Naver Band, and Telegram, zealously sharing information and encouraging the infected with promises they would get better soon. I've heard that among themselves they call him "President Shim."

You mustn't say things like that. It's thanks to his support, after all, that the villagers have been able to carry on all this time without a riot.

Professor Shim's facial deformity was so serious that he could no longer talk, and I'd heard his fingers were so swollen he couldn't type on a smartphone. He spent all day in front of the computer in his room, typing slowly with his thick fingers, sending texts and posting on blogs and running the community. And I heard he had an intense dislike for me.

It was unclear how Professor Shim was infected. He'd been making civil complaints here and there, saying that it's time for the infected to be released from isolation. Communications to that effect frequently reached the police substation. What could be more absurd?

The sergeant went on.

Identification of the body that was found in Okgye Port is coming in today. It's probably the last missing person we're going to get. On top of being very decayed, the disease ruined the tooth alignment and even the fingerprints, so apparently it took a long time to get a result.

I was about to reply with *Right,* but something hot surged up my throat. Suffering invades the village regularly, through the smallest gaps. If I look up from my work, it's always there, coiled, ready to attack.

What about my niece . . .

Things went quiet on the other end. A few times I saw him start to type a message, and each time it disappeared again. Sergeant Hyunjun was one of the few people who saw me break down like this.

I didn't even get to see the body.

I know. It was a chaotic time. There were false reports that corpses spread the disease, and no one was in their right mind. It was election time too, so the administration was a mess. They wouldn't act so rashly if it happened now.

I didn't even get to see her body.

As soon as the lockdown is lifted, you can find where she's buried and hold a proper funeral. Just sit tight. It has to end soon.

It'll be over soon. I heard that line three years ago.

At first, we just thought it was like a bad cold. When orders came from the government recommending everyone stay in the village for another week, Hyun pestered me to go out and see the sights. She was so excited she was rolling on the floor. Her parents said to obey the government, to come back when things had improved. And then the disease broke out. After a few days I found spots all over Hyun's body. The hospital I took her to was chaos, packed with patients. Within a few days visitors were banned. A few days after that, I was notified that she had died.

My older sister ranted and raved for days on end, howling that I had killed her baby. And then, at some point, after hurling a barrage of curses like she always did, she gave a deep sigh and said, "Well, in one way, it was fortunate. If I'd been the one to take her to Haewon, who knows, her dad and I might have caught the disease too . . ."

I felt a surge of nausea and hung up. We never contacted each other again.

Every night, my mind returns to Cheongnyangni Station. I imagine catching hold of Hyun's small hand as she races off. I imagine talking her down, reasoning with her.

"Something's not right, Hyun. Let's call home first and get on the next train. Let's play in the station for another hour."

"Something's not right. We can take a trip together anytime we want. Let's go home today."

"Something's not right. Let's change our tickets. We can go to the neighboring town. It's really pretty there too."

"Something's not right . . ."

Something's not right . . .

When I got to the beach a salty, rotting smell pricked at my nose. It was a familiar stench, but at the beach it became another level of awful. The air here is so rotten it clings. Mountains of fish carcasses have washed up on the shore. Piled in layer after layer, the fish press down on each other and putrefy, turning into mush from the bottom up. In the beginning, the villagers cleared the fish away somewhat, but now it's too much to handle. There are also countless fish flopping about, life still in them. After Haewon Port became a swamp of death, the fish that happened to drift into the bay couldn't get out, as though they'd been caught in a net. After circling around endlessly they must have felt so stifled. Must have decided it would be better just to come up onto the beach and end it.

Well, that's one way to explain it. One night I awoke from a nightmare and rushed, out of my mind, up Dawn Road in my pajamas. I clamored at the roadblock, shouting at the soldiers on guard that I was going home. I was quickly apprehended and taken back to the village. That night I lay face down among the dead fish on the beach and cried until morning.

Flocks of white birds cover the fish like a quilt, greedily pecking at their flesh. All around, plastic trash is piled as high as the dead fish. The plastic gets bumped around in the waves, breaks apart, and is worn down into small pebbles, and then the birds eat it, and the corpses of birds full of plastic pile up along with everything else.

The birds were sick too. The herring gulls of Haewon Village had unusually big, red eyes, and patches where feathers were missing. There were some that couldn't fly because the joints in their wings had bent out of shape.

As I looked out at the black craggy island backed by the sunrise, I was unconsciously scratching my forearm. It was bumpy with hives, reddened from being scratched. I looked through the sea mist to the dark cloud billowing at the rocky outcrop. Every time I see that cloud I am seized by fear. As far as I understand it, the dark cloud is formed when the rising air current from the blocked-off bay meets with cold air in the morning and evening. On the internet, people share memes about devil sightings on the rocky island.

The villagers don't go anywhere near the island. Most of the fishing boats in the village were smashed up in the maelstrom, but even families whose boats are still intact avoid the island and its shallowed waters, swirling torrents, and strong winds.

How long had I been sitting there like that? On Sunrise Road, a bus coated in dust sputtered its way along the coastline to a bus stop.

All the routes into the village were cut off, but that bus still drove its route inside the village twice a day, morning and evening, and took those with important business to the border of the village and back.

Getting off, I saw the village secretary who would go from house to house doing errands for people, and an old lady stooped low under a big bundle of spring vegetables, probably wages for day labor on a farm. And after them . . . I doubted my eyes.

An unfamiliar man sprung off the bus. He was a long way off, but I could tell he was clean and well turned-out, taking energetic steps into the village.

3

I would have been less shocked if a goblin had stumbled off the bus. I got straight up and strode toward the bus stop, squelching rotten fish underfoot.

When I got close, I could see the man peeking into a hole-in-the-wall store. The roof of the store had buckled to half its original height under the tidal wave, shorter than a person, and the buildings on either side had collapsed and just been left that way. Tapping his finger on the window reinforced with a tangle of tape, the man was shading his eyes to peer into the dark.

There were five other villagers close by, and all of us were watching him intently. The infected, with their hands gloved and cloth wound over their faces, must have been thinking the same as me. This man's sudden appearance was the biggest happening in the village for months.

The man brought his mouth to a hole in the window and raised his voice. "Hello! Anyone here? Is this place not open?"

It was a voice full of vitality, the likes of which you didn't hear in Haewon Village, even from children.

"The shopkeeper only comes out every other day," I said.

The man turned. Up close he looked about my age . . . somewhere in his late thirties. He gave off a soft, limp impression, like an office worker at a big corporation. His body was slender, and he wore a slick grey suit and towed a brand-new suitcase that didn't have a single scratch on it. His face was uncommonly good-looking, and his hair was neatly coiffed as though he had just visited a salon. His presence had no place in this village.

"Even when they're open, it's only after one in the afternoon," I continued, investigating the man from head to toe.

He looked pleased to see me. If nothing else, I don't show noticeable symptoms of East Sea Disease, aside from some blotches on my skin. To this man's eyes, I looked "human."

"Ah! Then might there be a supermarket around here? I forgot to pick up any cigarettes before I left. I'm so low on nicotine now I can hardly breathe."

"If you mean something like a local Hanaro co-op, it's been a long time since they closed down. There is another store if you go a few more stops on the bus, but . . ."

I was about to explain, but it was too much trouble. I stuck my leather-gloved hand into the flowerpot beside the door and dug the key out from the dirt. After opening the padlock that held the door closed, I tugged open a small flap that was just big enough to get an arm through. I retrieved a pack of cigarettes with a picture of a cancer-ridden larynx on the box and gave it to the man.

"Give me the money. I'll put it inside and close up again. Anyone and everyone puts their hands in there, so you'd better not."

Seeing the man's pale hand without a single patch of rough skin, again I felt the intense sense of something out of place. He was from the world the state protects, embraced and cushioned by the peace and simplicity of everyday life. I felt such envy it could make me tremble.

Having received his cigarettes, the man began chattering away.

"Is this—how do I put it—the rural way of doing things? I've only ever lived in Seoul, so, you know, it's my first time in such a rustic setting. Does everyone around here, ah, act like this?"

I looked around feeling uncomfortable. Our audience was now watching with great excitement, eyes fixed, as though they were seeing the latest film. My name would be on everyone's lips at the community center for days to come. It's not like I started talking to him out of my own curiosity.

"Why would someone from Seoul come to a place like this? Even setting foot in this village means you'll have to go through multiple tests and self-isolate for two weeks."

"Ah, well. I unexpectedly needed to get from Gangneung to Mokpo. But this week there's an extra-long weekend, with public holidays on Friday and Monday, so all the intercity buses were booked up. But while I was trying to figure out a route, I found that coming through this village made the timetables match up perfectly. Everything just clicked, clicked right into place, and there were seats available, too. Anyway, I'm the type who hardly leaves the house, so self-isolation is no big deal to me . . ."

As he talked about things clicking into place the man tapped his palm like a jumping grasshopper, but when he saw my expression, his face changed.

"Ah." He raised a finger. "This story isn't going to work, is it? I'll have to come up with something else."

He took an expensive-looking leather wallet out of his trousers pocket and handed me his business card. The wallet radiated the secure scent of a comfortable home.

"I work for an infectious diseases research institute. I'm on sabbatical this year, so I've embarked on some research for a paper. Did you know that there are mountains of papers written about Haewon Village, but only a tiny number of researchers have done on-site surveys? This year, it's zero. After submitting all the forms for getting permission to enter the village, I can see why! If I wasn't careful, I might have started filling out the visit application paperwork this year and not been able to come until next. But, anyway, I made it, as you can see."

I examined the man's business card front and back. The name "Ha Woojin" was followed by five official titles: employee of this company, member of that association and the like.

"Your accent tells me you didn't grow up here," he continued. "Are you from elsewhere? The local accent might not be as extreme as Jeolla or Gyeongsang provinces, but they have a funny intonation, don't they? That . . . dda ra lara? . . . raeyo? And the way they go up at the end of a sentence."

"There's a bus out this evening. You should leave right away."

He waved me off. "Is there anywhere to stay the night? Will I have to find the key in a flowerpot at the local accommodations too?"

I looked at Woojin, precious son of the Ha family line, and stayed silent for a moment, then tore out a piece of receipt paper from inside the store and scribbled a phone number.

"Go take a look at Sunup Guesthouse, on the coast road you see over there. The owner isn't always around, but they'll open it up for you if you call ahead."

"Is it clean? I'm not really the fussy type, but I'm a bit sensitive when it comes to bathrooms."

Again, I was silent for a moment. "They're operational. Listen, you need to go home as fast as you can. You want to become a super-spreader?"

Ha Woojin shook his head.

"Oh no, I've read all the research on East Sea Disease. This isn't a virus, it's a bacterial skin disease, and it's only mildly contagious, so a little short-term exposure is fine. People make such a fuss because of fears about deformity, not unlike with leprosy. Someone I know has volunteered for decades at the Sorok Island leper colony, and they're totally normal. No one's died from East Sea Disease outside of this village, and even inside the village, the data is contaminated by the environmental pollution brought by the tidal wave and the poverty that followed. These days, people are trying to trace the cause of death to water pollution or inadequate medical facilities, certainly not . . ."

Stopping midsentence, Woojin looked toward the beach, hand shading his eyes from the golden sunlight floating on the sea.

"What are those kids doing down there?"

I followed Woojin's gaze. In the distance, on the beach blackened with dead fish and plastic waste, a group of young people with their bodies coated in mud were dancing around a bonfire. It was early spring and our recent cold snap was still not over, but as if they weren't cold at all, they were half-naked, male and female alike.

"Is it some kind of local festival?" Woojin took out his phone, zoomed in, and began snapping photos.

The youth of Haewon spread mud on their bodies, to conceal the symptoms of their disease. They hide in the semidark of dawn and dusk, and sing songs and dance, reminiscing about a time when they were all just kids, all the same as each other. Mourning a peaceful life that has disappeared into the past forever.

"They're just the village kids. At some point that's what they started to do for fun. It's a long time since the school closed, and there's no indication that they'll be able to graduate. The stigma of being from Haewon Village will follow them for life, so they've no hope of finding work. Kids get bored with nothing to do, so they've gone crazy getting out all that youthful energy."

Snap, snap.

"And staying sane in a place like this is no better."

Woojin thrust a hand toward me.

"I think this must be a fateful connection. Would I be able to get an interview? Could I have your phone number?"

I stared down at Woojin's bare hand. It was only when he noticed mine, in black leather gloves, that he took some white cotton gloves out of his pocket. He pulled them on as if to say, "Here you go, I'm putting them on," and he put on a mask too.

I said, "The means of transmission of East Sea Disease are still unclear. You have to take precautions."

"I'm in the camp of people who believe there is no airborne transmission. And our side will win. I even put a bet on it. I'm what you might call a scout. *Pang! Pa-bang!*" Woojin said, pretending to fire shots all around. "I've come to carry out a preliminary investigation, so I'll only be here for a day or two. If you want to talk within that time, please contact me, you have my card."

Giving a nod to each and every one of the villagers who had been watching us, Woojin set off along the road, full of energy. I looked at the beach. The slanted sunlight flowed down the undressed bodies of the dancing youths. Those kids sometimes sing in a language I can't understand. It was a while before I learned that they're imitating the way East Sea Disease sufferers speak through their deformed oral cavities. The daughter of a shamanic family had taught her friends a ritual she learned over her parents' shoulders. She said the ceremony would console the dead people, the dead fish, and pacify the angered king of the sea. And comfort the tribe that emerged from the sea that day.

When I asked the kids what they meant by the tribe that came up from the sea, they told me that there were strange living things with human teeth and limbs sprawled on the ground in parts of the village devastated by the tidal wave. They said that the grown-ups had hurried to hide them away before outsiders discovered them, since things were chaotic enough without more bad rumors spreading.

There are, in fact, fish in the sea that have developed limbs like arms or legs to crawl along the seabed. With the volcanic eruption, rarely seen sea creatures from the deep ocean were swept onto the shore. People could imagine all kinds of things when they saw them, once the disaster had loosened their grip on reality.

4

When I arrived at the church, Mr. Jeon's flatbed truck was pulling up, sputtering away. It had been washed and disinfected, so the exterior sparkled, but it had been a long time since anyone had looked under the hood. Thick fumes spewed from the exhaust. Wearing a hazmat suit, Mr. Jeon greeted me as he got out of the truck.

"Well hello there, Marshal Seo."

Mr. Jeon used to call me "Police Officer Seo," but I corrected him a few times, explaining that I was not in fact a police officer. These days he calls me "marshal." Mr. Jeon had ordered himself a hazmat suit on the internet right before the village was put into lockdown. For the last three years he's worn that suit wherever he goes, even when he steps out to buy soju. When people mock him for being overdramatic, he responds with "Better to look stupid than get sick!" Even now he holds firm to his rule of never touching anyone. Maybe thanks to all that, Mr. Jeon became the only person allowed to enter and exit Haewon Village freely, and so he became the only means through which daily necessities make it into the village.

"Today I brought all the call number six hundreds. I'll give you a few before I stack them up in the village community center. Take whatever you want."

I helped Mr. Jeon untie the ropes and pull off the waterproof tarp covering the truck bed. The inside was tightly packed with dusty books. I picked up a few and browsed through them.

"Oh, they're science and technology books." I held up a thick textbook full of Chinese characters with both hands. "*Introduction to Aerospace Engineering*? What use is this to Haewon Village? You saying we should build an airplane to make our escape?"

"When you're cooped up inside all day, even the Yellow Pages can help pass the time."

Lately Mr. Jeon has been fixated on the books in the abandoned library of the now-shuttered Hanzhong University. The whole place was just left unattended and, being located on a quiet mountainside, it was easy to reach from the highway without having to go through the city. Mr. Jeon began by bringing in novels to loan out through the village community center. Now, as though getting carried away in all the excitement, it seemed he might end up bringing the entire university library into the village.

"Well, you never know. If things go on like this and the village is sealed up forever, the kids will still have to do some studying, even if it's by teaching themselves out of books. They'd have to do that much to become proper people, wouldn't you say?"

Mr. Jeon babbled on with the refrains he endlessly repeated. I picked out a few beginner-level books and put them in a plastic bag.

"Ah, that reminds me! Did you see the news yesterday? The director of Sarang Hospital's family is caught up in a huge corruption scandal, some embezzlement kind of thing."

"I haven't been online for a long time."

It seemed like he was going to go on talking, but Mr. Jeon just gave a shrug.

"I'm the same. I can't bear to look at it. Whatever site you go on, the attacks on our community are just too much to bear. People posting a photo of someone taking out the trash and accusing us of dumping illegal waste in the sea. Spreading a photo of neighborhood folk slicing up raw fish for a drinking party on the beach and saying we caught the disease by eating parasites. Anyone seeing that stuff would think we wanted to get sick."

Once the disease started spreading through the village all kinds of claims made the rounds online. In the beginning it was things that were regrettably true. They said the villagers were barely educated, or unemployed, or poor, and so they must have allowed the disease to spread unhindered through ignorant, unhygienic habits. After that the rumors completely detached from reality. That villagers are caught up in a cultish religion and throw chaotic sex parties every night, or that they gather at church on weekends to feast on rotten fish and fall into hallucinations. Photos went around of villagers' faces merged with monsters. In the span of a few years, the residents of this village were cast as a cursed breed of human, accused of all the hateful and disgusting things other humans could imagine.

All those ghastly stories really came down to the same thought: *Something like that could never happen to me.* Beyond a mere hope, it was almost a prayer. While mercilessly attacking other people with their rumors, in their heart of hearts they held a desperate wish. *Never let that happen to me.* That was what lay at the foundation of all of it.

Fear.

The horrifying fear that squeezes their hearts out of shape and makes their flesh shudder, day after day, with each and every step.

There was a poster stuck up on the church notice board, neatly handwritten with permanent marker, declaring "HOLY SPIRIT REVIVAL THIS FRIDAY EVENING! The Haewon of today was prophesied in the Book of Revelation—gain eternal life with your faith." The pastor's photograph that was reused every time a new poster was made, was stuck at the top corner. The church printer ran out of ink months ago, so by now the church elder who made all the posters had a lot of practice. Affixed on either side of the door were more posters, each in a different hand, reading "666, the mark of the devil appears, check the back of your family members' necks," "The Rapture is coming on the 31st of next month, only residents of Haewon village will rise to heaven, their bodies returned unscathed." These were put up by the leaders of minor denominations with less than ten believers each. The pastor let them use the church as a place to meet on the condition that they do the cleaning after their worship. There was something a bit cultish about the pastor himself, but he called them weirdos and reasoned that it was better if they were all gathered together in one place, rather than scattered around.

I went into the empty church, kneeled in front of the cross, and said a prayer. I'm not religious. I've never once believed in God. If there was a God, it would be proper for the residents of this village to hold a protest, not pray. But I'd been moved by the cunning evangelist idea that prayer is something you do for yourself, not God. So, I occasionally came in to meditate.

When I lifted my head, I saw that Ms. Jeong, the chief nurse at Sarang Hospital, was praying beside me. Nurse Jeong didn't have any symptoms of infection, but her eyes were sunken and she looked no different from a corpse. I felt sorry for her, watching time dry her to a husk. That's what happens when you have to fight a disease that never ends.

When Nurse Jeong's eyes met mine, she avoided my gaze without the faintest show of goodwill. We'd fallen out at some point, after I half blinded one of the delinquents who had broken quarantine. It turned out he was a distant nephew of hers. She had yelled at me, saying that I was roughing up the infected to deal with my own grief. There was nothing endearing about them. The infected that I've crossed paths with were mostly quarantine violators, and they all wanted me dead for putting them back in their homes.

"Work at the hospital is tough, isn't it?" I asked, pretending not to notice her coldness.

"It would all feel worthwhile, if only the patients showed some sign of improvement. There's still no news that they've made a vaccine, is there?"

I'd once seen a report that claimed the body can't build an immunity to East Sea Disease. A couple of days before that I had read an article saying that we would have to wait a few more years for a vaccine. And I saw a despair-inducing article that said the number of people infected was too small for the government to invest in an expensive vaccine.

"An article came out about the director's family embezzling funds, so the whole hospital is in disarray," Nurse Jeong said, her teeth clacking together as she anxiously gnawed on her fingernails.

Ah, the story I was just hearing about.

"One of the hospital director's relatives is a national assembly member, and he has an older sister who married into one of the conglomerate-owning families. He was using that connection to fill his pockets to bursting while violating every rule. Now it looks like we'll be audited, and everything is mayhem. They're destroying all the documents, anything that could be evidence, and it looks as though we'll even lose the patient records."

"Wha—that can't be right, can it?"

It was disconcerting hearing something close to a criminal confession from a woman I wasn't even friends with. It did happen to me now and then, but still.

"Of course, it's totally against regulations."

Nurse Jeong bit down on her fingernail. Her face looked more haggard than ever. A terror I couldn't fathom cast a deep shadow on her face, and I couldn't get it out of my mind.

"They say it's going to rain this evening," said Nurse Jeong.

"It might even snow, I heard. Don't catch a cold going out on rounds. Stay home today."

"Even if it doesn't, I worked through the night. I'm planning to rest."

"The service for the infected is about to start. We'd better get going."

When I looked behind me, I saw that people had seated themselves in ones and twos, their faces and heads and entire bodies covered with cloth. They all began to utter murmured prayers as soon as they sat down. Every one of them had their skin wrapped up in bandages, and wore cotton gloves and sunglasses, hats pushed down low on their heads. They looked determined not to bare a single inch of skin to the outside world. The right to worship was granted even to those under isolation orders, so they all showed up enthusiastically for their weekly church outing. Among them was a man with half of his face exposed, looking at me with cold eyes. It was difficult to identify him because of the way his eyes were deformed, but I recognized his denim jacket. We'd had a run-in before. A few months back I beat him to a pulp after he broke out of his home to get some beer.

People with East Sea Disease almost never blink. Moisture naturally gathers in the eyes, so their blinking becomes less frequent and then stops all together as their bodies dispense with unnecessary functions. Staring into those eyes that don't blink, with irises that don't respond to the light, a terror comes over you. It's like looking into the eyes of a corpse.

I left the church in a foul mood, passing a line of the infected making their way inside. Outside the doors I discovered someone I knew, and greeted her with excitement.

"Yoonhui!"

Kim Yoonhui, the second-generation Vietnamese woman I

met briefly in Cheongnyangni Station three years before. They say her mother married into the village and lived out the rest of her life here. When I had to settle in this village, unable to come or go, she had helped me, saying that she wanted to strengthen the tie we had formed in that moment. She helped me find a place to live and made sure I was getting by. In the village she seemed like a much more clever and strong-minded woman than I could have imagined, and we soon became friends.

Yoonhui was holding her husband's hand and climbing the stairs into the church with great care. Her husband had a severe case of the illness. His bones had developed growths that raised a large hump on his back, and his vertebrae protruded so much that you could count them through his coat. His arms were noticeably longer, and although it wasn't clearly visible beneath the bandages, the structure of his face was seriously swollen. His jawbone and teeth jutted out so far that his mouth couldn't close, and his bandages were always wet with saliva.

Without fail, Yoonhui accompanied her husband to the service for the infected. Having been subject to so much violence, day in and day out, it was hard for me to understand why she had chosen to care for her husband so devotedly, since he got sick and helpless.

"Muyoung."

Yoonhui seemed pleased to see me, but she scanned the surroundings before ushering me into a corner of the church, tugging at my clothes to bring me close.

"Muyoung, everyone's saying you beat Kim Sunja's boy half to death this morning," she whispered.

"I didn't kill him."

"Rumors about you have spread all through the infected community. Sunja's lot are fuming. You don't need me to tell you how much Sunja adores that kid."

"So I guess word didn't spread about how that little bastard wrung my neck and tried to kill me?"

Yoonhui looked around again, taking care that no one would hear us. "Stay home today, Muyoung. The weather is foul, and everyone's on edge. You might get caught out if you go roaming on a day like this."

It was still morning, and this was the third time since daybreak I'd been told to stay home. But I had no choice today anyway, I had to rest. I didn't get a wink of sleep, chasing that crazed kid around all night long.

Yoonhui's husband observed me silently, his back hunched. The arrogance I had seen in Cheongnyangni Station had completely vanished. He'd become so timid that, when I met him again, I thought he was a different person. It seemed the disease had wiped out his fierce temper. Or perhaps he had understood that, in his powerless state, he would die without his wife's care. While her husband's ferocious temper had died off completely, Yoonhui had become smarter and more assertive in inverse proportion. She also looked much healthier than when we'd first met, as though she was eating better these days.

Suddenly I remembered that there was a favor I wanted to ask Yoonhui, so I softened my expression.

"Um, Yoonhui . . . I heard you're going to be taking the boat out next week. I wonder . . ."

Yoonhui shook her head before hearing me out.

"I won't do anything," I continued. "I promise to be on my best behavior. Just take me, one time."

Yoonhui's family boat was one of the only ones to survive the storm, without even a dent. The sea all around had shallowed and the topography had transformed, with unfamiliar currents and spiraling torrents all around the rocky outcrop. Taking a boat out, even to nearby waters, meant risking your life. On top of that, as the water got more and more polluted, the catch dwindled to almost nothing. Even if they did catch something, there was nothing worth selling. If by some miracle, fish from Haewon made it to the markets, there'd be shoppers protesting in Gwanghwamun Square. Still, people in the village needed something to do, something they could feel they had produced for themselves. So periodically the villagers would select a fine day and take Yoonhui's boat out to fish, then distribute their catch to each family on their return.

Yoonhui spoke softly, "We take the boat out to catch fish, Muyoung. We don't go monster hunting."

I gave a flustered laugh.

"Don't be silly. That's not what I was thinking. I just want to feel the wind on my face, it's so stifling here."

"That reason is even worse. You know that almost every household in the village has gone to ruin since losing their income. There's no space on the boat to take someone out for a good time."

Yoonhui had good reasons for responding that way. It went back to the day I received news of Hyun's death. Sleeping alone in the damp room, I awoke around dawn gripped with fear. I was in the room where Hyun and I had stayed for two weeks. All around me were traces of a young child. The tangled scribbles Hyun had drawn, the colored paper she had folded into origami, the bedding that had gotten all creased by her rolling around putting on some imaginary production, even a half-finished carton of milk. I could see Hyun's specter in every inch of the room.

I crawled to the window where I could see the beams from the lighthouse and looked out at the sea. From the house located halfway up the mountainside I had a full view of the coast and the rocky outcrop. And I saw something there, on that jagged island . . .

I don't remember precisely what happened after that. When

I came to my senses I was at the wharf and was attempting to smash through the cabin door to Hyun's boat. I'd untied the ropes, and the boat was bobbing lose. People had me by my arms and legs, pulling me this way and that. Later they told me, I was screaming about there being a monster atop that rocky outcrop, and that it had taken Hyun.

"In a way, we all went a little bit crazy, didn't we?" Yoonhui spoke warmly. "We all went through things. It's not your fault, Muyoung. It's no one's fault. It was unavoidable. But even so, I will never take you out in our boat."

When she was done speaking Yoonhui went into the church with great care, supporting her husband with both arms, as though he were a precious treasure. I watched unmoving as Yoonhui placed a light kiss on his bandaged face and stroked his cheek.

Strolling aimlessly away, I noticed two young lovers kissing behind the church. The young man was infected, what looked like a mild case, and the young woman seemed to be untouched by the disease. The infected guy didn't have any hair left on his head and there were knobbly bumps on his face. But to the girl kissing him, it seemed her lover's appearance was insignificant, like it wasn't even visible to her.

Seeing the two of them together, I felt I had been abandoned by the whole world. When I put my hand in my pocket, I felt a crumpled business card.

5

In the Sea View Café even the tables by the window were filthy. The tabletop was sticky and the floor and chairs were covered with a white film of dust, as though the owner had opened without bothering to clean. For three years now, the place had been run with a self-service system. The owner shut himself in the kitchen, behind a small window like a ticket booth. Order slips went in, food and drink came out. The café was in a great location, but the scenery visible through the large windows was nothing but rotting fish and heaps of plastic now. The lemonade I ordered gave off a sour smell, and there were fingerprints and lip marks on both glasses. Feeling embarrassed, I wet a napkin and wiped at the glasses and tabletop in vain.

Ha Woojin showed up at the door, turning his head this way and that. Discovering me, he gave an enthusiastic wave. The dreary interior of the café seemed to brighten as this man set foot inside.

"Did you find the guesthouse OK?"

Woojin answered yes, yes, and noisily pulled up a chair. He plunked into the seat, fanning his face with his hand, then gulped down half of his lemonade in one go. It occurred to me that he was the kind of person who made every place they stepped into noisy.

"I had to walk along the main road for ages, since there are no buses or taxis to be seen. The place is worse than I imagined. The wallpaper is damp and blistering off the walls, spiders crawling across the floor, and the water in the toilet comes out black. The doorhandle is out of order, so you have to double-fasten the door with a bolt, but even that pops out of the doorframe if you give it a pull. If someone made up their mind to get into the room, well, they'd have no trouble at all."

He spoke with such energy. Now that I could examine him thoroughly, he was even better looking than I'd thought earlier. His gut didn't stick out, his height was just handsomely tall, and he had well-defined features. For so long, all I'd seen were the infected or people rippled with wrinkles from the wear and tear of the salty wind. Sitting across from someone all sleek and smooth with city water in their veins was dazzling. *Does he have a family*? I wondered. *A wife or kids?* Such thoughts flitted through my mind out of nowhere.

"The owner of the guesthouse is seriously depressed. She said I was the first person they'd seen all year. Not even first customer, but the first person! Would you believe it? Well, if that was the case, you'd think she would treat me well, but in the ten minutes it took for me to get set up with a room, four times over I heard the refrain 'Looking out at that swarthy sea I feel so suffocated I could die.' When it came time to pay, she slurred, 'Fiddy thousand won,' so I handed over fifty thousand. She said, 'Uh, siddy thousand.' Well, you won't see me putting my life on the line for pocket change."

He probably has a retirement account. And three or four different insurance policies. He must be doing some investment trading. He'll go around on days off checking out real estate. He lives with the firm belief that tomorrow will continue on like today, and next year will flow on like this year, never doubting for a moment that the whole of society is working flat-out to ensure the peace and comfort of his lifestyle.

I changed the topic. "Did you carry out any interviews?"

"The owner of the guesthouse seemed as though she couldn't understand me, but I was able to have a short conversation with an elderly man who was sitting outside the fire station like a faithful wife who turned to stone while waiting for her husband. Aside from his rants about divine punishment from the wrathful sea god, it was worth listening to. Ah, don't get me wrong. It was interesting, but not useful in any way. He seemed to believe that his friends and family and other villagers had been replaced by gilled monsters that came up out of the sea. I can see how an elderly person spending their days in such surroundings could get to feeling that way. And then I got your phone call and rushed right here."

Done with his speech, Woojin looked me over.

"How long have you been in the village?" Having thoroughly examined my skin and features, Woojin gestured at the baton and army knife hung clipped to my belt. "Were you sent here on a work assignment, or as a volunteer? You know, something like that?" He used broad motions, as if I would struggle to understand him.

"I'm one of the unlucky tourists who got trapped here. I didn't have any other way to make a living, so I got special authorization from the police, a bit like a neighborhood watch."

"Ah! Catching thieves and that kind of stuff?"

"Everyone in the village knows everyone else, so it isn't really like that. I mainly track down villagers who break their quarantine orders and put them back in their homes."

"I see," Woojin shrugged, no interest in his expression. "The reason I ask is just, your face, uh . . ."

"Looks normal, right?" I cut in. "They thought I might have some kind of antibody and took a whole barrel of my blood for testing. They must have taken samples of every part of me, everything I was wearing, everything I touched. But nothing's come to light yet. I'm just one of the lucky ones. None of us know how long that will last, trapped in here with the infected. We can't hold out forever."

"Shouldn't the uninfected be allowed to leave?"

"They say that's not possible because the means of infection are still unknown. We might be asymptomatic carriers. I understand it. If the infection starts spreading outside the village, the whole country will come to a standstill."

A shadow came over Woojin's face. As though a thought had just occurred to him, he tapped anxiously on his glass. He kept checking the surroundings, like what he was about to say was something that no one else must hear.

Woojin hunched over and lowered his voice. "As I was on my way here just now, I happened to see an infected person's face . . ."

It was like he had learned a terrible secret, and that keeping it to himself was too much to bear. His breathing sped up, hot on my face.

"After getting your call, I saw two of them that looked like mother and child walking along the coastal road hand in hand. I gave a big wave and went up to greet them. You see, I had some strawberry chocolate in my pocket. I wanted to win them over and get an interview. But when the girl saw me, she stumbled and fell. As the mother struggled to help the girl up, a gust of wind snatched off the cloths that had been wrapped over their faces."

With an expression of pure horror, Woojin clutched the glass of lemonade and chugged it down like beer. As he worked at calming his breathing, he loosened his tie a little.

"The moment I saw them I lost all my words. I felt as if the blood in my body had dried up. My hunch that no one has been doing research in the village was certainly right. The little thing had no hair at all, not even the trace of hair follicles that you often see when someone has shaved their head. Just smooth skin.

It was catching the sun and glistening. Abnormal growth in their neck bones forced their necks out forward, and I could see bumps protruding from their spines. I knew that elevated eye pressure was a symptom, but both of them had serious facial deformities. Their jawbones were protruding like those of a fish or a frog. Their lips were stuck pouting and open, and a layer of pus had formed beneath the exposed oral mucosa. Their skin was like that of a dead fish, and had all these splotchy markings . . ."

Woojin's voice had been rising bit by bit, but when he saw my expression he went quiet.

"Forgive me. I was just so startled. I'd seen pictures, but in real life, well, it was a whole different thing."

"It's OK, it's hardly surprising. Seeing them for the first time is a lot to take in."

"It is alright for the diseased to be walking around with such severe symptoms? What happened to the isolation orders?"

"It's the weekend," I said. "They're allowed to go to church."

"I suppose the bacteria must check their calendars and say, 'ah, this is a day of rest.'"

The isolation requirements were being gradually relaxed anyway, starting with those with mild symptoms. With everyone stuck at home, they would die of poverty before the disease killed them. For people to keep on living, someone somewhere has to work, bring in necessities, and get things done.

". . . they looked as though all the evil of the world had been concentrated into their ghastly forms."

The moment I heard this, a heavy stone settled into place on my heart. The goodwill I had felt toward this person, the flutter of nervous excitement I had felt wondering if I should ask if he had a partner, a family, it went cold in an instant.

"I couldn't describe them as anything but devilish. As though they'd come up from the depths of hell . . ."

"Ugly, aren't they?" I cut him off. "The residents of this village became ugly. But there is no correspondence between ugliness and evil. One is no indication of the other."

Woojin abruptly disengaged and crossed his arms, staring out the window with a defensive expression. He looked offended.

"I suppose that's true."

At last, I clearly saw the wall around this sleek-looking man's heart. I got wise to the fact that he was the type who knew nothing of the world except what was inside his own head. That he was the kind of person most accustomed to speaking for an audience who nodded along to everything he said. I folded up my slight attraction, and set it aside. But it had been so long since I had chatted with someone who wasn't depressed or despairing. I decided to put up with the predictable arrogance of a well-off man for a while.

Woojin got out his smartphone and tapped away. Judging by how he used two fingers to zoom in and out on the screen and kept ogling out the window, he must have been studying a map.

"Oh, you've got the same model as me," I said, holding up my phone.

"Ah. I don't upgrade mine often either." Indifferent, Woojin continued, "They send all the East Sea Disease patients who need treatment to Sarang Hospital, don't they?"

"Only because that's where they sent them in the beginning. No one wants to contaminate a second hospital. It's not a big hospital, but there's no other way."

There's no cure for East Sea Disease, but there are treatments for the symptoms. In unlucky cases skeletal deformation can put pressure on internal organs or even cause rupture and internal bleeding. Facial deformity can cause breathing problems too. Although only a small provincial hospital, Sarang was designated an East Sea Disease specialist center, but this wasn't exactly a case of selecting the best option, it was that all the patients were already there. The inpatients who had been at the hospital before the disease were forcibly discharged, and the people living close by held protests for a long time afterward, demanding compensation for their loss of healthcare and livelihood.

"Are the facilities and medical staff up to standard?"

"We have to hope they are. It's totally off limits to anyone who doesn't work there."

"Yesterday the news was full of reports about a corruption scandal involving the elder brother of the hospital director. Did you see them?"

"I heard."

"Apparently there was misappropriation of funds, and even just the cash they found in his home was a formidable sum. Everyone knows that doctors are rich, but where could he have gotten all that money? And so there are rumors going around that the hospital director must have taken all the government funding without providing proper treatment to the patients."

It was only then that Nurse Jeong came to mind. The desolation that had descended on her face, something more than just the stress of overwork. By now the hospital director may have destroyed all the records, got a plane ticket, and made a break for it. What would happen to all the patients in the hospital?

As an anxious feeling swept over me, a Kakao Talk alert rang out from my pocket. It was Sergeant Hyunjun.

About the body I mentioned this morning. Something's off.
I'm sending over the documents now.

"When I was on the bus coming here, I was looking through a book on the history of the leper colony at Sorok Island." While I was scanning through the files in Kakao, Woojin began babbling.

"The hospital directors in the early days were highly respected, and patients were gathered together with the best intentions. But they say that as Japanese imperial rule persisted, subsequent directors carried out horrific abuse. Eventually, one of the patients killed the hospital director. It was murder, but since the victim was a Japanese colonial official, it could also be considered an act of resistance. When liberation came three years later, the patients protested, demanding their autonomous rights. Do you know what happened?"

I looked up at him.

"The Korean workers at the facility killed eighty-four of the patients. They buried them in a mass grave. The lepers were buried alive and set on fire. They didn't think of them as human. They were just people who got sick, with a disease that happened to make them ugly, that's all."

I assumed at first that he was deploring how people could commit such atrocity, but I could feel an oddly different intention lurking in his words. As though he was saying that this was the way humans naturally are, trying to justify his fear as instinct.

I looked down again, and no more of what Woojin said reached me. The identity verification document Sergeant Hyunjun had sent over contained a name that couldn't possibly be there. I hurriedly typed a response.

Are they sure it's him?

That's what the paperwork says.

But that can't be true.

Strange, isn't it? If it's true, who's the person that always comes to church? Who have we been meeting, and greeting, and talking to all this time?

6

As forecast, dark clouds began to roll in from the sea. By four in the afternoon the day was already gloomy as night.

Yoonhui's doorbell was dead. It was coated with a film of black slime, and there was lichen growing from under the button. It looked as though no hand had touched it for a long time. Yoonhui's place was a two-story wooden home, peeking up between vegetable fields and greenhouse tunnels, down in the part of the village that had flooded. The surrounding homes had been left smashed up, and only this home had an embankment built around it, its roof mended, its walls set right. The exterior walls were damp, and all the paint was blistering off. A thick mat of ivy clung to everything, even the windows. The front door, cracked like an old tree, had a rusty sign that must have been put up by the authorities in the early days: "Infected Resident, Keep Out." Yoonhui's husband had never broken the isolation orders, and so I had never needed to come here. When the doorbell made no sound, I banged on the door.

I heard someone coming down the wooden staircase. The footsteps sounded more like dragging than walking. Amid silence, the solitary creaking felt eerie. Each step was long and slow. It made me imagine Yoonhui descending from some impossibly distant place, not just the second floor.

The door opened a tiny crack with the safety latch in place. Yoonhui brought her eyes to the gap in the door and peered out.

Did she live with the lights off? Out of the darkness of her home only Yoonhui's keen eyes emitted a chilling light.

"Muyoung! What is it?"

"I'm here for work. There's something I need to ask your husband about."

I showed her the photograph I kept on my phone of a police badge with the police chief's seal on it. It was laughable really, but this was agreed-upon practice in the village.

"This is the home of an infected person. The uninfected mustn't come in. Let's meet another time at church."

I shook my head. "It won't take long."

"Didn't you say you'd stay at home today, Muyoung?"

It hit me in a rush of feeling: I was an outsider. I didn't say I would stay home. It was this person, and so many others, who told me to stay home. Don't go roaming outside. Why did everyone want me to stay home today?

"Let's meet up another time, somewhere else," Yoonhui said. "I haven't cleaned, and the place is a mess."

A fishy odor exuded from within. It was a heinous stench, more than enough to overpower the odor that wafted through the whole village. I had to wonder if they kept boxes of rotting fish in there. As Yoonhui made to close the door, I forced my hand in through the opening.

"Are you crazy?" Yoonhui screamed. "What do you think you're doing?"

She tried to pry my fingers from the door, but I'd spent too long in daily scuffles with crazed men. I stood like a rock and looked in at the dim interior. All the lights were off. I felt as though I was peering inside a tomb. I put my foot against the wall for leverage and used all my strength to pull the door open. The rusted latch popped out of the mushy wall and fell with a thud.

I pushed Yoonhui aside and turned on my phone flashlight.

The state of the inside was even worse than the exterior. It was as though someone had left the house to soak in dirty seawater. Cockroaches scattered away from the light in all directions. There were fungi and barnacles growing on everything and silverfish had burrowed holes in the walls, wriggling below the surface. Black mold thrived on the damp curtains and there were maggots floating in a rice bowl left in the sink. Wherever I trod, water squelched out of the linoleum and the floor sunk beneath my weight. There were tangled waterweeds stuck to the floor, and in a sloping corner some had put down roots and were growing strong.

It's seawater, I thought, observing the wretched state of the interior. *They're splashing seawater all over the house. On the walls, the floor, everywhere. Maybe every day.*

"It's . . . because of my husband," Yoonhui's words faltered. "He needs humid air. His skin splits if it's even a little bit dry. He likes the humidity, and the doctor recommended it too. There's no way of getting a humidifier around here, so . . ."

A loud creak sounded from above. The noise was far bulkier than the one Yoonhui had made coming down the stairs. I bound up the stairs to the second floor.

"The house is in such a state," Yoonhui yelped after me. "I don't want you to see it . . . ! Please leave! Get out!"

I flung open the bedroom door. The person inside froze in shock and turned to look at me.

No. It wasn't a person.

For the very first time, I was encountering the form that had been hidden away under layers of fabric. The bulging eyes of Yoonhui's husband—no, the thing that may once have been her husband—were fixed on me. Eyes that swelled to cover half its face. Jawbone protruding like a frog's, neck lined with wrinkled folds. On the hump of its curved back was something which could only be described as a fin, and it was wiggling. The creature had translucent webbing on its hands and feet, and its body was green like rotting leaves, with black splotches all over its skin. Where ears should have been, there were gills excreting foam as they flapped open and closed.

There was a huge, shallow basin set in the middle of the room, and it was full of dirty seawater thick with weeds. The monster was just lifting its body out of it. It was naked, hurriedly putting on a shirt. Based on the evidence, there was no doubt as to what the two of them had been doing. This was Yoonhui's husband. And a husband who, for some time, she had been living in harmony with.

Khi-nli-rik khi-rik. Khi-rik.

The monster made a threatening gnarl. Its neck swelled up large and it bared its needly teeth. Having observed the bizarre creature's muscles hardening, my hand moved like lightning to the holsters on my belt. It was not my baton that I grabbed instinctively. *I knew today would be the day.* The beam from the lighthouse that came in through the window reflected off my knife with a cold gleam.

Yoonhui rushed in and grabbed me from behind, using all her weight to keep me in place.

"Darling, stay calm . . . Muyoung, please . . ."

The skin pressing on my back was damp. A body that hadn't yet dried. Until a moment ago, Yoonhui must have been tumbling around in that basin with whatever this thing was.

"Muyoung, darling, don't we greet each other at church all the time? Why are you facing off like strangers?"

"That . . . is not your husband," I said, not loosening my grip on the knife. "Your husband is dead. His rotting body washed up at Okgye Port a while back. I just received the paperwork. I don't know what that is, but it's not your husband."

"You're right. He isn't."

Veins bulged on Yoonhui's fingers. The fact that it was me, not that thing, she was using all her might to restrain, made it clear who she wanted to protect.

"We eat and sleep together, how would I not know that?"

Still showing its hostility, the creature stepped back. It looked as though it felt perfectly well. It wasn't suffering from skeletal abnormality or deformity, no skin conditions. It wasn't sick. It was a flawless specimen of whatever it was, a species that looked like this from the beginning.

"It's not one of the other infected, either. That thing was never human."

"Right, that's true. But he's . . . a really kind person . . . he came up out of the sea on the day of the flood."

I had to keep myself from turning to look at Yoonhui, make myself face my opponent.

"After the tidal wave tore through the house, I ran down from the village in a state. I saw everything all smashed and broken, and my husband was nowhere to be found. There were traces of blood on a shattered window, so I think he must have been swept out through that. Instead of him, this guy was in the yard . . . He was injured and in pain. Gasping . . ."

The sound of the creature's breathing softened, and the tension in its muscles eased. It was my body that was gradually stiffening with horror.

"The people who came down here that day, they saw it all . . ."

"What did they see?"

An unsettling excitement came to Yoonhui's eyes.

"From out of that sea . . . ancient people, who lived on the seafloor, in the deepest depths . . . they were swept up in the ocean current and brought all the way here. If we hadn't helped them, they wouldn't have survived."

"Help . . . ?" It felt as if my blood was drying up. "Who? Who else helped them? How many people know about this? How many more of these things are in the village?"

"He's a good person, Muyoung. He's kind and polite, and he doesn't hit me," Yoonhui said. "Please, just leave, pretend you saw nothing. If we stay in this village, I can spend my life with this person. I love him. I'm happier than I've been for years."

I heard another voice from behind. "Oh my god, oh my god . . ."

As Yoonhui's grasp loosened, I jumped and turned around. Woojin was standing on the stairs, trembling as he held up his phone, photographing the creature. I looked past him to see that the door was blowing this way and that in the wind. Damn it, he must have followed me from the café.

"No . . . no one will believe it." He was muttering, babbling. "Who could have imagined . . . My god, ho . . . horrendous . . . m-monster . . . monster!"

Instinctively, I moved to block the camera with my body. "Stop! Put the phone down." This horrible thing was the shame of Haewon village, and that made it my shame too. Although I wasn't yet sure about the details of this strange affair, it was a scene I would never, ever want outsiders to see.

Before I could reach Woojin, I heard an ear-splitting sound from behind. It was a sinister, horrible shriek that seemed to come from the depths of hell.

Flipping over the basin, the creature sprung up and rushed at Woojin. Water gushed noisily down the stairs. The creature knocked Woojin down and climbed on top of him. Pressing down his limbs, it opened its mouth wide. It was an angle that human jaws could never open to. Its face split in two like that of a crocodile. Inside the creature's mouth were a multitude of sharp, spindly teeth, like those of an angler fish. Facing this open mouth, Woojin screamed and writhed like a fish. All the blood left his face, and it was as though the color was fading from his hair.

No matter the shame to the village, I had to protect Woojin from this creature. I flung my body against it and tried desperately to get it off him. But, like a boulder, the creature didn't budge. It had a strength that went far beyond what I could have imagined. Had it been an act, all this time, tottering like someone frail and infirm? Or was this creature unable to gather up strength in the dry air? Barely seeming to notice that I was hanging off it, the creature sunk its teeth into Woojin's neck. Woojin screamed endlessly, as though he was caught in the devil's jaws.

The creature's maw took in more than half of Woojin's neck. Its sharp teeth were latched on. If I pulled it off by force, Woojin's neck would be ripped apart. And if I did nothing, he would be torn apart just the same. There was no time to waver. I had to decide.

. . . I guess today was the day.

I brought my knife down on the creature's neck, aiming for the carotid artery.

This time a despairing, pitiful scream sounded behind me.

The creature's skin was hard as stone, so the knife's point turned. I jumped up on its back and pushed the knife in with both arms, leveraging all my weight. Once the skin parted, the inside was soft. The knife passed through the creature's neck and out the other side. The creature's body jerked, and then it sagged, and at last it spread like water.

How long did I wait there like that? Only after it went limp did the tension in my body release, and I flopped down on the floor panting. When I pried the creature's jaws open with both hands, beads of blood sprouted from the dense line of pricks on

Woojin's neck. It mixed with the dark blood pouring from the monster's mouth.

"U-aah, u-aaaah, u-aaaaaa!"

Woojin squirmed and tried to crawl away on his hands and knees, screaming all the while, but there was no strength in his limbs. He slid around helplessly. With a wrestling pin, I held Woojin's struggling body down between my legs and took off his tie to wrap around his neck. Perhaps thinking I was about to strangle him, Woojin writhed even more pathetically.

"Stay still! If you can scream, it means your windpipe is intact. Get to a hospital! You might have been infected!"

I tried to tell him that ambulances wouldn't come to the village, so he would have to make his own way there. I was ready to convince him, tell him we don't know if the monster would transmit the virus like the infected . . . but it seemed he couldn't hear anything I said. Everything inside this man, his intellect, his hold on life, all the things that keep a person together, had been vaporized by fear. As soon as I got off of him, Woojin cried out like prey that had gotten free of a trap, and scuttled down the stairs on all fours.

That's going to cause trouble. I had to send a message to Sergeant Hyunjun and ask him to take care of it. Get him to the hospital for testing . . . But how to make sure he wouldn't speak of what he saw?

That last thought made me stop. Not speak of it? What was I trying to stop him from saying?

As I was writing the message, I felt a gaze from behind like a pickaxe. It was only then that I turned around. Embracing the creature with her whole body, Yoonhui was glaring at me as if to cast all the curses of the world on my head. She was smeared with the creature's blood and her eyes, burning with loathing and resentment, were fixed on me as she embraced the stretched-out creature, gathering it up in her arms.

"There was no other way," I spluttered. "If I hadn't intervened, it would have murdered that man. I'll file a report with the police station. You'll have to do some explaining."

I felt like I had become the last person in the world hanging on to a scrap of reason when everything had been torn apart. I deliberately averted my gaze from the monster that sagged limp as fish skin. The fact was, I wanted to be able to say that I had encountered a monster and disposed of it, as a representative of humanity facing an alien enemy. But, from the depths of despair, Yoonhui's eyes seemed to say, *If my husband had looked human, whatever the circumstances, if he had looked even a little more human, you wouldn't have killed him like that.*

Yoonhui spoke. It was a low and dismal sound that I had never heard from her lips. The most desolate sound I had ever heard in my life.

"We . . . we were . . . looking out for you, Seo Muyoung."

"What's that supposed to mean?" I asked, straightening up. "Looking out for me? Who's 'we'?"

"You were one of the enemy, Seo Muyoung. One of those who mistreat and torment us. I was doing all I could to protect you."

"'Enemy'? Who's the enemy, aside from me?"

"I was right out in front, protecting you. Me, protecting you. Risking myself, for you. I held them back with all my might. I made sure that no one would touch you. What a fool."

Yoonhui let out a groaning sob. Her bloodshot eyes grew redder. Her stained teeth showed terrible in the darkness. Yoonhui wrapped her whole body around the creature, as though she wanted to become one with it, as though determined to remember even this last waning warmth.

"There won't be anyone to look out for you now, Seo Muyoung. No one in this village will show you goodwill."

What could I say to that?

"If you want to save your life, you'd better get out of this village before morning."

7

I staggered out of Yoonhui's house. My insides flipped and I wanted to throw up. Drizzling rain swirled around me. As the wind picked up, waves crashed noisily on the rocks.

Enemy. I kept thinking about that word. *Enemy* and *us*. Someone, some group Yoonhui is part of, had divided the village into two categories. Into *enemy* and *us*. And Yoonhui said that I was an *enemy*. In that case, who else is an enemy?

I heard a dismal cry from the rocky islet. I tried to believe it was a flock of herring gulls all calling at once, but I couldn't ignore the evil shadow within that sound. It was a chilling cry, that seemed as though it could freeze down to the bone.

When I looked, I saw a dark dense cloud rolling from the islet. Stunned by a fear that struck like lightning, I stared at the dark cloud unable to move a muscle. I was sure that something over there was watching me. Even if I were to ask what it wanted from me, all I'd get back was the howl of the wind. I felt as though the whole world had turned its back on me. That cloud could envelop me in an instant and hurl me into the sea, and I'd die in a moment, unnoticed, unmourned.

A Kakao alert jolted me, a message from Sergeant Hyunjun. How long had I been standing there?

I rushed straight to Sunup Guesthouse like you told me to. That man from the city, he'd shut himself in his room. I

heard him shrieking over and over. I asked if he was alright and kept knocking on the door, but there was no response. He just kept making that sound. I was so worried that I got the key from the owner and opened the door. He was packing, but his hands were shaking so much that half the things he picked up slipped out of them. When he saw me, he screamed and started convulsing. I guess my face must have frightened him. He hurled his case and everything in it to one side and jumped out the window.

Ah shit, what a mess.

I'm worried for him. The weather is awful. He needs to get to the health center, so they can administer a sedative or something. I've told the other neighborhood watch patrols to look for him too.

Enemy. That word circled in my mind. Is Hyunjun an enemy, or one of them? If the police and the neighborhood watch are the enemies, then . . . what is going to happen to the enemy tonight? Should I warn Hyunjun to be careful, or should I hide what I've found out?

Did you go to Yoonhui's place?

Sergeant Hyunjun's message made me jump.

Did you meet her husband?

I wasn't sure how to respond. Afraid that he could feel my hesitation through the screen, I hurriedly typed a response.

Not yet.

That makes sense . . . it's late after all. We have to assume the report was wrong.

I paused for a moment.

Hyunjun, I heard something strange just now . . .

What is it?

That day, when the tidal wave swept through the village . . . have you ever heard people say something like . . . that a different species came up out of the sea?

It felt ridiculous to bring up such things. There was no way it could be true. But I wanted it to be true. The thing I had just seen, it couldn't be human. It absolutely had to be something else. If it was human, then I had just committed murder. Without hesitation, with no remorse, as if I were doing something that naturally had to be done. And for that reason, I needed that thing not to have been human.

All was quiet across the screen. I saw Hyunjun typing a few times but nothing came through. It occurred to me that I should have done this via voice call. A video call might have been even better. I regretted bringing it up. With written messages I had no way of knowing what Sergeant Hyunjun was thinking in the moment. Whether he was laughing at me saying something so ridiculous, or hiding his gloomy expression and trying to come up with lies.

Enemy, us.

Yes, there are people who say that.

Hyunjun's message appeared. Raindrops tapped on my phone screen.

They say their family members were swept away in the tidal wave, and an ancient species crawled up from the deep sea to live in their homes with them. I've seen a few people who genuinely believe that. I think it's called mass hypnosis? If one person believes something with all their heart and they keep claiming it's true, in time other people also follow along with them and start believing too. No matter how strange the thing is. I can understand why villagers would want to think that way. Having to face the terrible way their loved ones transformed, wouldn't it be easier to accept the idea that they were replaced with a different species?

It was only then that it occurred to me that, actually, I had heard such talk before. It was just that every time I heard it, I shrugged it off. I started to feel like I knew nothing.

You must be exhausted. Go home and take a rest.

I was shivering from the chill of the rain seeping into me. I pulled my knife from the sheath on my belt. Drops of rain slid down the blade. While I stared at the red coating the metal, the knife was rinsed clean. The moment the blood disappeared, I doubted my memory. I closed my eyes, opened them again, and wrote a message.

Why do you keep telling me to go home?

The response took a while.

Because you must be worn out. Did something happen?

Adjusting my wet clothes, I held my jacket over my head and hurried toward home.

I couldn't get out of the village, so my plan was to shut myself up indoors. If I stayed put tonight, nothing would happen. All the scary stuff would run its course while I was asleep. Without any grounds for thinking that, I hastened my steps.

I turned into the narrow alleyway that went up to my house on the hillside. It was lined with stone walls, and only one person at a time could pass through. A dark grey gull, its feathers patchy, flew toward me and perched, then flapped off. Up the hill in the gloomy distance, someone stood blocking my path.

Their face was wrapped in fabric. Their body was huge, their back was hunched, and their bandaged arms hung limp at their sides. One of the infected. A serious case who must be prohibited from going outside. I tried hard to believe that this person just happened to be going the other way, and stopped because the alley was too narrow. But they stood stone-still. I carefully observed the huge bolt cutters they held in one hand. Raindrops dripped from the metal to the ground.

When I turned around, two more people appeared at the other end of the stone-walled alley. One of them was Jean Jacket, who I had seen earlier at church. Three infected people breaking isolation.

The person blocking my way slowly removed the fabric covering their face. The ones behind followed suit. Through the heavy rain, I saw faces marked by round, bulging eyes and bumpy growths. I couldn't tell whether the person ahead was a man or woman, their gender or their age. But instinctively, I knew who it was. Professor Shim Yeongho. The leader of the infected. Their spiritual pillar. The one who had kept their spirits up, maintained order, and kept them at home for three years without a riot.

Ah, then I understood.

The doors of hell were opening tonight.

The day had come for all those who had lived in hiding to emerge, to show their hideous forms to the world. The time had come for the *us* to hunt their *enemy*.

I pulled my knife, gripped it tight. I stood side-on, so that I could fight back an attack from either direction, tracking their movements with my ears. The driving rain on the roof tiles was noisy, but it wasn't enough to hinder my hearing.

Professor Shim made a bizarre sound. It wasn't human language. It seemed his oral cavity had been completely transformed. If I tried to write it down, it would be something like, "Ph'nglui mglw'nafh Cthulhu R'lyeh wgah'nagl fhtagn . . ."

From the other side, Jean Jacket said: "Seo Muyoung, we will give you a chance to join us. Come with us."

He must be acting as the professor's interpreter.

"A chance? What chance? Where are you taking me?"

"You'll know when you get there."

"Go bother someone else," I replied, gripping tight to the knife in my hand.

A narrow alleyway that only a single person could squeeze through. I would be able to face them one at a time. At the very least they couldn't take me down without a fight.

Professor Shim spoke more incomprehensible sounds and held his free hand out to me. The interpreter repeated, "Come with us, Seo Muyoung. Let's go together. We'll show you."

8

After sundown in Haewon Village, you can't see an inch in front of you. There are no shops open at night, no streetlights on the road, and no boats going out with lamps to fish.

The three quarantine breakers lead me to the waterfront. Past the quayside with its deserted maritime police station, we walked along the sand and gravel paths far from the road. The waves wet my shoes and they soon grew heavy. Thinking that I wouldn't be able to run like this, I threw away my socks caked in wet sand and carried my shoes as I walked. Although I trudged along slowly, the three of them just watched, never rushing me.

Unperturbed by the bad weather, there was an altar fire burning on the distant Haewon seawall.

Whenever we strayed close to some homes or a larger road, I looked to see if anyone was around, if anyone would intervene, but there was no one. For the first time, I thought about the proportions of the infected and uninfected in the population of the village. How many uninfected people were left? It occurred to me that villagers might be huddled around the windows of every house, quietly watching me pass.

The three of them crossed over the coast road and began to climb the mountain. Twigs and fallen branches stabbed into my bare feet, so I had no choice but to put my shoes back on, heavy as rocks.

I wondered where they were planning to do me in. No, I'd

be lucky if all they did was kill me. Please, let it be that easy. I tripped on a rock and fell. I thought that my body losing balance would be a signal for some kind of attack, but my watchers just waited quietly. I still had my knife and baton hanging at my waist. Why weren't they taking my weapons away? Maybe they weren't worried about such trivial things.

It was only when we were halfway up the mountain that I realized where they were leading me. When I caught sight of the building from a long way off, I began to tremble from my core. It was Sarang Hospital. The place where, before anyone knew that East Sea Disease sufferers needed moisture and cold, the first of the infected had suffered and died. The place where Hyun was admitted, but never discharged.

We approached the hospital from behind. It was encircled by a barbed wire fence covered with signs saying "quarantine zone," "keep out." Professor Shim stepped out ahead, cut open the fence with the bolt cutters, and went inside.

When we got to the employee entrance at the back of the hospital, Nurse Jeong opened the door from the inside, wearing a mask. My three escorts went straight inside, not even greeting her.

I glanced at Nurse Jeong. Her expression showed that she'd known I was coming. Her eyes said it all. *You're not one of us. What you do next will determine whether you live or die tonight.*

Having entered the hospital, comprehending the scene unfolding there took all I had. The doors to the isolation wards were wide open. Working in unison, the doctors and nurses were removing the bandages that covered the bodies of the infected, taking out their IVs, and untying the cloth restraints that had been holding patients to their beds. The infected bared their deformed faces and walked out together. But their unsightly faces weren't all that frightening. It was the scene at the end of the corridor that made me freeze.

The hospital director was prostrate, tied up with rope and covered in blood. It looked as though he had taken multiple blows to the head with a blunt weapon. One side of his skull had caved in. I met him a few times at church. He would preach with his eyes closed tight, swaying and bowing like a balloon man outside a store's opening day, saying, "I believe that our Lord Jesus Christ will drive the sickness away." He had an appealing presence and came across as a gentle person. That same person now had his eyes rolled all the way back, his tongue hanging out, and had been discarded like a piece of trash. I didn't take my eyes off the corpse. I tried to set the precise details in my mind, for fear that my imagination would make it even more horrible.

None of the patients showed the least interest in the hospital director's corpse. It seemed they all knew about it already. The murder was old news, unanimously condoned.

Jean Jacket pushed me from behind and gestured with his chin for me to move. With my mouth tightly closed, I glared at him, but did not budge.

"Move."

I didn't. What reason was there left for me to endure such humiliation? My end was already decided. What was I going to achieve by continuing to follow the whims of these ghouls? Why should I amuse my murderers for a moment longer?

Jean Jacket pushed me harder and I almost fell down. He continued to push, until I lost all resolve and followed like a dog. Patients joined us, and we moved forward in a crowd. For the most part they were silent, and when they did speak, they conversed in a language I couldn't understand. It seemed they had made their own new language.

I was led down to the basement. I kept feeling waves of fear that made it hard to breathe. I was sure that I would soon faint, fall flat on my face. As I descended the stairs, a foul fish odor stung my nose. That stench that I had encountered at Yoonhui's house: the moist, clammy smell of the rotting sea.

In the basement there was a thick metal door. It was locked by an iron latch and chain. Judging by the traces of newly applied cement, the structure had recently been reworked. I saw that scattered around the door were aluminum pots with dried food on their bottoms. At the base of the door was a small hatch that looked like a cat flap. My eyes must have deceived me. Looking at the cat flap, I thought I saw a hand dart out and grope about the floor before disappearing back inside.

Professor Shim murmured beside me, and Jean Jacket interpreted. As though it were impossible to precisely convey what was being said, the words were dry and blunt.

"The hospital director was planning to set fire to this isolation chamber tonight and make a run for it. He thought he could get out of the village by hiding the true symptoms of the disease. He thought that if he reported the situation as it was, the government would never let him leave. He convinced the hospital employees that this was what they had to do.

"They hid the patients with the most extreme symptoms in here. They assumed they would die before long, but actually, the humidity and darkness kept them alive.

"We know full well that the disease won't kill us. We merely become something different.

". . . just like they did," Jean Jacket added for himself.

Professor Shim cut the lock with the huge bolt cutters. Multiple people had to push before the metal door finally moved.

I saw something that had been crouched by the door shoot out like a bullet. It scrabbled through the aluminum pots, searching. It wasn't human—it couldn't possibly be human. There was a fin sticking out of its back, gills rising and falling on its neck.

On the other side of the door were stairs that led down and

down. It seemed the space had been reshaped and repurposed multiple times. Water leaked down walls that were covered with black mold. The floor was soaked. Creatures lined the stairs, their bodies wrapped in dirty fabric that couldn't be called clothes. I realized that the strongest among them commanded the spots by the door and had been getting all the food.

The farther we descended, the more we saw of hell. On the soggy wet floor, former patients were tangled up with corpses. Other creatures were picking at food among corpses, self-respect forgotten, nothing left to lose. Shallow metal bunks stacked high like a charnel house were all that was provided for them.

I was looking around, and then I froze. It felt as though my body was being struck by a hammer.

I stumbled through a puddle, shaking uncontrollably. The tiny figure was huddled in a corner, wearing a tattered headband. Her face was completely unrecognizable: her skin was dark, and her teeth stuck out. But I knew the faded red headband on the little head that had lost all its hair. Her clothes were grimy, but there was pink lace sewn to the bottom of her skirt. Falling to my knees, I took the headband in my hand. As though determined not to let this one thing be taken from her, right away the young thing snatched the headband back.

Out of my mind, I wrapped my arms around the child. It was only then that, instead of pushing me away, she fell into my embrace.

"Aun . . . di?"

Speaking words I couldn't understand, the child hugged me. She had grown much taller in the years that had passed. Her skin glistened green, and a white webbing showed between her fingers.

The ones who had brought me here quietly observed as I embraced Hyun and sobbed. Professor Shim made a gesture, and with that they let me be and got on with their work. It seemed they had concluded that I was neither the *enemy* nor *us*, but no more than a pitiable woman.

I sensed that people were beginning to leave in ones and twos. They had been confined in this terrible place for such a long time, but they didn't push each other, or squabble to get out first. They were all quiet as ghosts. None of that mattered to me. The cold life that was in my arms once again was all there was.

9

I practically burst down the door to my house. I lay Hyun down in the bedroom, wrapped her in a quilt, and, not knowing what it was I had to protect her from, I locked the door and closed all the windows. I looked at the state of the place. The house was cleaner than that basement, at least.

The kid will want to see outside. They kept her in the darkness. Ah, she needs a warm bath. I've got to turn on the heating. There should be a new bedding set in the attic. Where did I put her warm clothes?

I rushed around, tripping here and there, as I chased the urgent tasks that kept coming to mind. It was only after I had gotten the new bedding down from the attic and spread it on the floor, and gotten new clothes out of the suitcase that hadn't once been opened in all that time, that I realized Hyun was standing up and looking outside. She had wriggled out of the quilt and crawled to the window. *She must have missed the sea*, I thought. Something unbounded. Whatever it may be.

I hugged Hyun from the back. Her body was cold and slick as a corpse. I stroked her head, and the sparse remaining hairs fell away like lint. When Hyun let out a purring breath it gave off a rotten smell like decomposing leaves. It's alright. It's all fine. What does her hair matter? No one who lives here is much to look at. Let's just, never leave the village, and live here for a thousand, ten thousand years. If we do that, we'll be alright. It'll all be fine.

"What are you looking at?"

When I asked, Hyun lifted a swollen, elongated finger and pointed out of the window. I looked outside.

Burning torches appeared one after another in the dark streets. The windows and doors of every house were opened wide. From this house and that house, one alleyway and then another, people were emerging. There were people whose family members opened the door for them and others who came out of their own accord. As the infected escaping the hospital returned to their homes, houses that had been dark for a long time glowed bright. All of the people in the street were removing and discarding the fabric that had covered their faces. There were some who had taken off all their clothes, exposing their naked bodies. Mottled bodies filled the streets. I hugged Hyun tight.

This is it, the day when all the doors open, I thought, my face buried in Hyun's back. *The day when all those who had lived in hiding come out into the world.*

Hyun wriggled in my embrace. She squirmed out of my arms and started toward the door.

"Hey Hyun, where are you going?"

Hyun gestured outside and pulled at my hand. She looked like a tiny animal that had nothing left in it but innocent instinct. She opened her mouth and said something, but I couldn't understand. I tried to lip-read, but I couldn't read her deformed mouth. Hyun kept speaking without letting up, as though she believed with certainty that I would have the capacity to understand her.

"I'm sorry, Hyun, I can't understand," I said regretfully, trying to pull her back and sit her down. Hyun kept moving toward the door.

"Hey, you should at least have a bath before you go. Change your clothes if nothing else. You've got to eat something. Auntie will make you some rice. I'll mix an egg into it for you."

Hyun shook her head.

"I have to go. My family is there. My friends. I belong with them," she seemed to say.

As though drawn by magnetic force, I followed Hyun outside. The rain had eased off, but the wind was still fierce.

I walked along, trying hard to shelter Hyun's body with my arms and clothes. It was only much later that it occurred to me that this weather was better for the infected; it energized them. As we passed out of the stone-walled alley and began to descend the hill, the number of people with torches grew and grew. From every street corner, I could hear the sound of people murmuring each other's names after a long time apart. They all touched each other's deformed faces and hugged.

When we arrived at the black seashore, villagers were gathered under Professor Shim's guidance, holding up their torches. I knew that, mixed among them, there were members of a completely different species. Complete organisms, neither deformed nor infected. Things with green skin and fins and webbed paws. I had the thought that, mixed among the infected, they had probably looked after them so that the transition wouldn't drive them mad; so that their minds and bodies weren't ruined. They must have taught them the laws of a different world, and showed them how to live life in changed bodies. Stayed to guide and comfort them.

I held onto Hyun with both hands. To protect Hyun, yes, but also to preserve my own safety. No one lay a hand on this child, because I am beside her. No one lay a hand on me, because one of yours is my companion.

Standing on the coastal road for a long time, watching things unfold, I spotted groups of the strange creatures approaching from the opposite direction, bearing long, fabric-wrapped bundles on their shoulders. The long-dead bodies were set down at the seashore in ones and twos. The creatures took their time. After placing one down, they would go bring another from who knows where. And in the darkness there was a splashing. They were pushing the corpses out into the sea.

This is a funeral, I thought. *They're holding a funeral.*

These folk that came up from the ocean floor. They had been huddled indoors for all that time, like caged, wild animals, and the thing that they most longed for was not food or a warm bed. It wasn't even freedom. They wanted to hold a funeral for their dead. They wanted to mourn those who were lost.

Just then I heard a shutter tone from close by. The sound of a phone camera snapped the bizarre illusion spread out before me in an instant. Turning to look, I could easily spot someone attempting to hide between two houses, repeatedly photographing the scene.

Even in the darkness, the person stood out. There was no one else around with such an unscathed appearance, in no way deformed or distorted. His expression was resolute. You could feel a determination from him, like that of a reporter who has pledged to put their life on the line for the human race. I couldn't recognize him straight away. Within the space of a day, his face had gone completely wild.

"Woojin?"

As soon as I called his name, he went white with fear and began convulsing.

"Are you alright?"

When I took a step toward him, Woojin screamed and crawled along the ground. A few people looked our way, but they didn't take much interest. It occurred to me that he might have been afraid of Hyun's appearance, but I wasn't about to let her out of my arms.

"Woojin, you don't look good . . ."

Woojin struggled frantically, waving his hands as though trying to rub everything from his vision.

"Guh, guh, get away! Get away, you hideous monster! Go, you devil! Be gone!"

That was when it happened. A sound like an explosion jolted the village. The echo reverberated off the hillside and the buildings and echoed back from far away. One of the people on the sand furthest from the sea crumpled like a dry leaf. People nearby who hadn't yet realized what was going on continued to mill around. A person who had bent over to try to wake the one on the ground crumpled down too with the splitting cry of another explosion. Their flaming torch tumbled onto the sand.

The word "gun" rang out among the gathered crowd, along with the slap of the waves. Screaming all the while, the crowd dispersed like a flock of birds. They trampled rotting, gas-swollen fish underfoot, making them pop.

From the other side of the coastal road, substation commander Jeon Sucheol was yelling and firing off shots. His face had turned purple and his eyes were stretched wide with fear. Acting out of desperation, having lost all sense of reason, he was shooting randomly without even taking aim, reloading right away. He looked like a crazed vigilante who had discovered a swarm of monsters from an alien planet occupying his backyard. Instinctively, I held Hyun tight and pulled my knife. I felt her turn her body and cover me in her embrace. With a *p'i-yung*, a sharp wind brushed against my body.

Thank goodness, I thought, *the bullet only brushed past*. But at that moment Hyun became heavy and her weight pulled me to my knees.

Hyun swayed like a gentle wave and collapsed. At first I thought she was just drowsy, fighting off sleep. Just like in the train station. That was what I wanted to believe. Hyun clawed at my arm and then pulled me into a tight embrace.

Out of the corner of my eye I spotted Professor Shim running, practically on four limbs. His speed far exceeded that of a human. His muscles were swollen almost to bursting, and the teeth cramming his jaw tore open the skin of his face. Bullets pierced his body, but he didn't stop. The professor pinned down the substation commander with his heavy body, bit into his neck like a lion, and shook. I watched him feed on the substation commander, mauling his prey. The gunshots continued, mingling with terrified screams. The rattling clack of the hammer went on for a long time and then finally slowed to a stop. Only then did the professor's superhuman, beastly energy gradually calm.

Hyun didn't even cry much, only clung onto me to the very end. As though to leave no doubt that she had lived through all her hardship for that one, slight movement at the right moment. I held her right back. Where did my child learn to die? Who taught her that one day, life ends and never comes back?

While I was holding Hyun, thin, high-pitched laments sounded from all directions.

I was oblivious to my surroundings. How long had I been there like that, collapsed on the sand? A shadow was cast over me, and when I looked up I was surrounded by four of the creatures. Not infected people, not deformed humans, but perfect organisms, the things they were born to be.

Smelling their muddy scent of death, I waited without knowing what I was waiting for. Then, all of a sudden, I realized that it wasn't me they wanted but Hyun. They wanted me to hand over their friend, their family member.

"Never! Leave us be!"

I hugged Hyun tight and hunched over her.

"I won't give her to you. Get away!"

They waited without a word, as though they could stand there for an eternity if that's what it took. No, please. Not unless you take me too, to sink with her beneath that rotting sea.

I slowly began to realize, though, that this child belonged to them. She was no longer mine, no longer part of the world on land. She had to go to her new home, back to the sea.

All strength left my hands. The creatures wasted no time and pulled Hyun out of my arms. Dark blue hands lifted her up by the arms, legs, and neck and carried Hyun away. I balked as though I'd just been stabbed, then grabbed her from them and curled my body over her.

As I bawled and shook, they waited again. Hyun was theirs, and they knew it. But they knew, too, that I had earned this time. They could wait just that long, but they would never leave her with me.

"We'll give you the time you need to say goodbye," they seemed to say. "But this does not belong to you. The child is one of our kind now. She comes with us."

I clung onto Hyun until I was barely conscious, but in the end, my body gave out and collapsed on the sand. With all reverence, the creatures lifted the child out of my lifeless arms.

The last creature to remain knelt before me and took hold of my hand. It felt cold, slippery and damp. Their glistening eyes, huge and unblinking, looked into mine as they whispered something I could not understand. "R'lyeh fhtagn . . ."

What was this creature trying to tell me?

Had I been wrong? A thought occurred to me. *What if, maybe, this wasn't a funeral?* Just as moisture and cold helped their bodies thrive, what if seawater cured them? What if, in that dark, deep sea, they could even be revived from death?

"Hyun . . . Are you taking Hyun to revive her?" I squeezed the creature's hand. "That's it, isn't it? So she can live? That's why you're gathering the bodies of your kind, isn't that right? And that's why you're taking Hyun too, right? To live with you in your underwater kingdom. Isn't that so?"

The creature carried on speaking in a hushed tone, but didn't tell me what I wanted to hear.

"Answer me," I howled. "Please! I need to know!"

But the creature must not have understood what I was saying, just like I couldn't understand them. It patted the back of my hand and left me.

I watched from a distance as the procession reformed and headed toward the shore. I looked on helplessly as my child accompanied those creatures deep into the rough black sea.

10

The rites continued late into the night. Even after the last creatures disappeared into the sea, the people who remained didn't leave the beach. Youths who had covered their bodies in mud, lovers and families who hadn't met for a long time, they all sat huddled together with no thought of leaving.

Blasted by the cold wind, I was forgotten, discarded, alone by the sea. The rain picked up, and in the cold night wind, rain became snow, and snow and hail mixed, pounding my body bitterly.

I itched all over, as though my skin was teeming with bugs. Having lost everything, there was no need for me to temper the urge to scratch. My nails tore into my skin. I continued to scrape at patches raw and bleeding. My eyes itched unbearably. Then, something occurred to me. I raised my head to look out at the rocky islet towering from the sea.

Beyond the beach heaped with trash and fish corpses, beyond the undulating sea gloopy as rice porridge, on the rocky mountain that had reared its dismal head like a huge beast, there rose a dark shadow. I saw it clearly now. Some vast body was on that island, twitching, lumbering, alive. With eyes that seemed to contain unfathomable depths, it was watching me. The monster.

Above its long beard, I read the message in its eyes. "You are as insignificant as the fish carcasses scattered on that beach. An insignificant, meaningless thing, no more than a speck of dust that deluded itself into thinking it was born with meaning.

Now you are going to your meaningless end, oblivious to why you were born and lived and went through agony and held onto desires and flailed in struggle. You will never exist again and will leave no trace on the world. Your life or death makes no difference. Just by encountering me today, your mind, your body will all shatter and become nothing. No different than the child you tried to save today, or the child of mine you killed."

More than the fact that I was facing an ultimate being I couldn't fully fathom let alone influence, my heart was frozen solid with the certainty that the vast being contained no transcendent spirituality, no sympathy or altruism, not even a vague philosophy about how the world should be. That being would claim my life and gain nothing from it, not pleasure, not anything, with the indifference of a raging storm. With no regard for the life I lived.

The hailstones fell harder. Just then the phone in my pocket vibrated. I took it out and stared at it for a while before I registered anything out of the ordinary. This familiar object did not belong to me. I had picked up this battered phone from the ground without a second thought in all the chaos, assuming it was mine. I began looking through the contents and became engrossed in reading a plethora of official-looking documents I had never seen before, all the while being pelted with snow and rain.

I felt an unsettling presence from behind. I heard a low, dismal sound that wasn't human. Looking up, among the snow and hail falling all around, I had been surrounded again by three of them. Monsters with gills, webbed feet, and fins.

Why are they still here? Aah, right. I guess these jerks must still have work to do. Since the *enemy* is still here. An *enemy* who has taken the life of one of their kin.

I understood. It made sense. Tonight, all human laws had

crumbled in this village. Everything was unfolding according to their laws, not mine. But understanding and accepting were separate issues. I shoved the phone back into my pocket, and shoulder-tackled the closest creature. As it fell, I started to run.

I fled up a narrow winding alley that climbed into the village. On a cement stairway one of them launched itself onto me with its mouth open wide. I looked the monster right in the eye and stabbed my knife deep into its calf. The monster rolled on the floor clutching its leg and I continued up the steps, almost crawling. Another monster scrambled over its colleague and ran at me, grabbing me by the ankle. I stabbed its hand and kept running. *Seems like you stinking fishlords haven't learned how to use your limbs properly out of the water. Well here on land we have tools too. How about that?*

As I turned into another alley a different creature blocked my path. I kicked a stone cairn that was piled up beside me and it came crashing down. My apologies to all the wishes made by the devoted people who piled stone after stone here. As the creature shielded its head, I turned and rolled into an empty house. The clatter of footsteps passed by outside the door. I crouched down into a ball.

A miraculous silence settled. It couldn't last long. I put my jacket over my head so that no light would seep out and turned on my phone.

There were a ton of messages and missed calls from Sergeant Hyunjun.

Muyoung, it seems some patients have escaped from the hospital.

Compared to what I'd been through, the message was so simple it felt completely divorced from reality.

It's an emergency situation so I've requested backup.
Stay at home, or if you're outside right now, come straight to the station. I'll protect you.

Enemy, us, enemy, us . . .

I lowered my head. I gave up on thinking. Which side he was on didn't matter. Let's just believe he's on my side. That would feel a bit better.

With a hunch that it would be a final farewell, I sent a message.

Take care, Hyunjun.

Muyoung? Nunim? Where are you?

I blocked Hyunjun and made a call to someone else.

It rang, but no one answered. I'd expected as much. I waited until I heard the words "Leave a message after the . . ." then hung up and called again and again. After a while it sounded as though someone had picked up, and then the line went dead. I called again.

I heard someone pick up again. This time, instead of hanging up, there was silence. Through the cracked phone gushed loathing as deadly as poison. It felt as though the hatred in that silence would dry up my vitality and kill me.

"Yoonhui, it's alright if you don't say anything, and it's alright if you curse me, but whatever you do, don't hang up. I'm going to send you a document. You need to open it, please don't just delete it."

Hailstones pounded the slate roof. I took a different phone out of my pocket.

A crab scuttled out of a cracked plastic bowl, and a mouse scratched its way into a corner. The phone I'd found had gotten wet, and my hands were cold and damp, so it didn't respond to my touch. There was only one bar of signal, and the battery was running low. I turned the phone here and there and wiped the screen with my sleeve over and over, pressing hard to get a response. When it finally began sending documents to Yoonhui, the progress bar was still for a long time. A low sigh sounded from my own phone.

". . . come to my place. I'll hide you here," Yoonhui said.

Please send. It's fine if you never work again, but send, please.

"Once the night is over, the people who started all this will be rounded up. You can hide out until then. Come and shelter here."

No.

"It's not that . . ."

". . . Just come. When all is said and done, the living have to live."

The moment "sent" popped up on the other phone's screen, that phone died. A moment later, Yoonhui ended the call. All strength drained out of me. I collapsed, almost hitting my head on the wall. It's done. I won't move again. If a monster comes in through that door right now, that'll be it.

After a long time, my phone rang. I tried shaking it but the screen was dead so nothing came up. Whatever punk removed buttons and receivers and dials from telephones surely didn't get into heaven. I guessed where the slider to answer a call might usually have shown up and swiped. I heard Yoonhui's voice.

"Muyoung, what is this?"

I had picked up that scuffed phone from the floor thinking it was mine. When I looked inside and found the documents, formatted like reports, I realized it was Woojin's. It seemed the frontal lobe of that enthusiastic young researcher kept functioning, even after the rest of his brain was laid waste. Or maybe the fact that he had written so many reports in such a short time was clearer evidence that he had lost his mind.

The documents contained extensive and detailed descriptions of every scene and event he had observed in the village. If you were to erase all the superfluous additions like "bestial" and "risen from the depths of hell," or "unforgettably terrible," "dread that could stop your heart," "nightmarish," and "evil-shadowed," the content was pretty close to the truth.

Fear had grabbed that man by the hair and shaken until everything was mixed up. In every sentence that fear raged like a storm of hatred toward the entire village. Every document ended with such stupid sentiments as "strengthening of quarantine is required," "if they cannot be contained, the army should be deployed to suppress them, or else supplies cut off to induce starvation," "control of media necessary." Judging by his call history, this man with a tiny lump for a liver had experience in seriously influential roles including, astoundingly, as an aide to a national assembly member. Based on the fact that he hadn't used a fake business card, this man was, at the very least, someone with connections that reached into the upper echelons of state power.

"Yoonhui, make sure that man, Woojin, doesn't get out of this village." I was shocked by my own words, but I went on. "That man's story mustn't get out. Our version has to get to the outside first. Use the excuse of treating his mind and body to hold him up somewhere. If needed, restrain him by force. I have his phone, so he won't be able to contact anyone."

I finished what I had to say and curled up, clutching my head. Haven't I done enough now? God damn it, whatever higher power is out there, isn't this enough? Haven't I hung onto my mind longer than could ever be demanded? Please let me go, set me free. If I've clung onto my mind as it rampaged as ferociously as a wild beast for this long, surely God, or something, should come down and reward me?

My wet clothes stuck fast to my skin and the cold was seeping into my bones. I shouldn't have given Hyun up. Even if we were thrown into the sea together, I should have stuck by her until the end. If I'd done that, the last straw of my spirit would have remained intact at least. I wouldn't have to be feeling this emptiness.

A while later, I woke to my phone ringing again.

"That man . . ."

"I spread the word to catch him," Yoonhui cut me off. "Anyone looking that clean-cut in this village will stick out anywhere, so he'll be caught in no time."

I had nothing more to say.

"Muyoung, come to my place." She spoke with a much kinder tone than before. "Oh no, our home would be a bit scary, wouldn't it? I'll go to you. If I'm beside you, there's no way you'll be hurt. I'll protect you, just for tonight. I can do that much."

I shook my head. I burst into tears and couldn't speak properly.

"Yoonhui, can . . . please, let me . . . use your boat."

"Muyoung, this isn't a day when we can launch the boat. And it's no good trying to escape by sea. The coast guard patrol near the village, and . . ."

"It's not about escaping. You know why."

Yoonhui was silent.

"Please, let me go . . . I beg you . . ."

I'd descended into such madness, who could possibly understand me? But, perhaps, each of us in our respective madness could begin to comprehend the other.

After a long silence, Yoonhui responded, "Come to the dock at Haewon Port."

I waited until I heard there was no one around, then stepped out. Hailstones slid off the slate roof like small beads, and fell on the stone steps, piling up in heaps at the corners. The dandelions and new shoots that had only just sprouted from between the rocks were wilting in the gusting cold.

I checked my surroundings with eyes blurred with tears. The lighthouse on the mountainside was silently illuminating the village, as though all was well, as though it had seen nothing. Haewon Village after nightfall could be distinguished from the outside by the lights. On the other side of the mountain, neon signs streamed like stars, while this side of the mountain was shrouded in gloom.

In the middle of it all I noticed a pack of people coursing someone, like hounds after a hare. Out at the very front, a man was sprinting for his life. Even in the darkness, Ha Woojin's sleek white shirt and shiny grey suit stood out. I wondered whether Woojin's terror or the villagers' loss of reason had begun the chase, but what did it matter?

Good luck, you pathetic man.

11

At the dock, where the waves swirled and crashed, Yoonhui had come out alone covered with a ripped plastic rain poncho and was starting the sputtering engine. The fishing boat, fluttering in the waves like an autumn leaf, already looked like it was about to fall to pieces. Nearby spread the shattered wreckage of a few small boats that had been rotting, eaten away by lichen.

A boat isn't something that floats on water by nature. I remembered the refrain I had heard from the villagers. In the wind and rain, the undulating waves can form unexpected curves, lifting boats up high then sending them crashing down. A sailor charting a course into wind and waves is no different from a sparrow flying into a typhoon. Without saying a word, Yoonhui helped me onto the boat. After letting me take the wheel, she matter-of-factly informed me of the basics.

"This red dot is the boat. The red line is your direction of travel. Keep to that line. Listen carefully. If a wave comes, meet it head-on. It mustn't hit you from the side. And make sure you don't turn the wheel too fast. If you remember only that, the boat won't flip over."

Yoonhui didn't bother telling me how to anchor or turn the boat around. She knew that I had no intention of coming back. I nodded, only half paying attention, staring all the while at the island. Hold out just until there. It's fine to sink, but we have to get there first.

A round windshield wiper spun like an electric fan. The propeller turned, churning up the remains of dead fish. The half-rotten stuff tore like tissue and turned to mush.

Standing on the wharf, Yoonhui sent me off in silence with a look that seemed to say, "What does it matter if it makes sense or not, how can anyone change the mind of a person set on walking straight into hell? I guess it'll be a different hell to the one she's lived in. A new hell, if nothing else."

The waves rose higher than the boat, and tumbled down across the window and onto the deck. With a crash, something collided with one side of the boat. I didn't care to check on it. Even if the boat did take on water, it only needed to make it a little way.

As I approached the islet, the rash that had come out on my arms spread rapidly up my neck and onto my face. Red boils appeared on my body, blistered, and burst. My eyes hurt as though they were about to pop, and my scalp felt ready to peel right off my skull. The pressure in my eyes expanded my pupils, transforming the scenery around me. The darkness that had obscured everything gave way, and my surroundings became rainbow-colored as though fireworks were going off in every direction. The driving rain became indistinct and the sky shone so bright that I had to squint. The sea scattered dazzling light in a kaleidoscope of colors. The strange rock formations of the craggy islet stood out so clearly it was as though I could reach out and touch them. The scene was resplendent, more brilliant than anything I had ever seen.

And there, looking my way with its arm draped around the rocky outcrop, I saw it: the vast mountain of a being.

Its body spanned my entire view of the sea. Its sleek skin was coated with ooze, and a fin and webbed flippers and feathers and wings stuck out from its towering body. In its bottomless and unfeeling eyes, there was an abyss like the darkest depths of the sea.

That thing must have been there since the day the volcano erupted and the sea was wrenched out of shape. It merely couldn't be sensed with shabby human senses. We'd stayed oblivious because the light it emitted was outside the visible spectrum. But the fish, the birds, the insects, and the shellfish all knew. That's why they chose to gather at the coast and die, unable to bear the terror. Those whose bodies changed with the infection must have known too. When they opened their eyes in the morning, they would have been able to see this thing standing outside their windows. A being that would drive you crazy, make you flee, make you end your life, or fall to your knees in worship; its terrible presence allowed no other option, no other way to survive.

Right, I had known all along. A smile came to my lips, and I mumbled with perfect certainty, "It was you who spread this plague."

The disease poured from your body, from your indifferent spite. You lingered there to transform us into your kind, to increase the subjects of your kingdom. Be gone, you monster. Go back to where you came from.

A crash shook the fishing boat, louder than last time. I could hear the bow smashing. Blackened water gurgled and gushed into the cabin.

With the boat breaking apart all around me, I shot toward the colossal monster.

12

Ha Woojin
PhD in Biochemistry, ████████ University
Researcher, Korea Contagious Diseases Society
Budget Consultant, National Treasury Support Initiative for East Sea Disease Sufferers
Director, Association of Intellectuals for Protecting Humankind from Ancient Species
[REDACTED]

Your Excellency the President,

After I made a narrow escape from Haewon Village, I ran to the nearest police station. At the station they threatened to send me to jail or a psychiatric hospital. Who could blame them? Later, when I examined the photograph they took at the station to confirm my identity, I saw how fearsome I had looked. I couldn't even recognize myself in the mirror. My hair was disheveled and it had turned white overnight, so I looked about twenty years older than I was. Having witnessed such abominations, my eyes had sunken into my skull, and my clothes were torn to rags. One of my shoes was missing, but I hadn't even noticed. I'd made it all the way there on a bloodied foot. I heard later that I had splayed out on the floor of the police station and screamed, foaming at the mouth, that Haewon Village must be quarantined forever, and that if it couldn't be cut off, the residents should be wiped out with missiles. Then I passed out, and when I came to, I took up screaming all over again. I loudly proclaimed that I had evidence, and handed my phone over to the police officers, but it was nothing but a wet pack of cigarettes. Clearly the cultists must have stolen my phone and had it destroyed.

But I saw it all, with my own eyes. Those ghastly monsters, the sinister rites where the believers send human sacrifices into the sea, to worship their fearsome god from the bottom of the ocean that revealed its detestable form on the rocky islet.

After I escaped the village, I was unable to set foot outside the house for months on end. Whenever I fell asleep, I would suffer nightmares of the monsters hunting me, and wake screaming that a devil was coming from hell to kill me. Within those few months, I lost over forty pounds. I am now only skin and bones, so frail that I cannot leave my bed. I foresee that, before long, this horror will take the last of my vitality from me and I will die.

Gathering all my remaining strength, I have been submitting civil complaints to every institution that may be able to intervene. The district office and city hall, government agencies, the courts, major media outlets. I even contacted a whole host of popular scientists, in the hope it could make some difference. I didn't hear back from most of them. It seems likely that the influence of those monsters has spread throughout the government.

A few media outlets have requested an interview, but when the articles came out, most of what I told them had been sanded down or distorted. Their articles merely say that the director of the local hospital was illegally confining and abusing the infected, and that he died at their hands before he could kill them to destroy the evidence. By focusing on the hospital, they miss the most significant parts of what went on.

Ah, every time I think of the events of that day my heart pounds like crazy, and my hands shake so violently that it's hard to type.

A couple of days ago I saw a newspaper article about Haewon Village. After reading its hideous distortions I was so enraged that I rang the news desk and lodged a complaint. How could someone with a medical degree utter such ludicrous statements? In the article, it said that East Sea Disease does indeed cause skeletal abnormalities, facial deformity, and the excretion of a strong odor, but it does not threaten human life. It claimed that aside from needing moisture and cool temperatures, the villagers are very healthy. It said that transmission didn't occur between humans, but rather that infection arises from unidentified bacteria buried deep underground that was brought to the surface when water levels changed. They had statistics that purported to show that, after a fire occurred on that islet when a sailor crashed a boat into it, the geothermal heat subsided, and there have been no new occurrences of the illness since. Accordingly, it called for the quarantine of Haewon Village to be lifted and the villagers who have been through such hardships to be accepted back into our society.

Your Excellency, please believe what I must tell you. This can never be allowed to happen. The volcanic eruption and the flood brought to the surface an otherworldly species that had been living in the deepest depths of the sea. The people in that village lived alongside them, had aberrant intercourse with them, rubbed flesh against inhuman flesh. Now they are giving birth to young that will become a new species. The monsters have taken advantage of East Sea Disease to replace dead villagers. They have gone into their families and are living among them. If the quarantine is lifted, their filthy genes will be mixed into the blood of our human race like poison. Their monster DNA will mix with ours like microplastics or synthetic chemical compounds and circulate within humanity for eternity. Imagine a distant future, when it is not humans living on earth but a teeming mass of glistening, writhing forms, more amphibian or reptilian than human.

If only I could impart this horror to someone, anyone! By spending just one day in the pit of hell, lured there by my childish sense of adventure, my life has sunken into the depths of despair. Until I hear with my own ears that those horrors have been completely burned out of this world, there will be no end to my agony.

Government organizations and the media didn't listen to me, but my efforts have not all been in vain. There are over ten thousand members now gathered together on my Daum server, people who support my work. My supporters overseas are also growing in number. Five different satellite groups have been formed by server members. They are all brave people who do not compromise their principles and keep fighting despite threats and baseless rumors. Through YouTube and in-person conventions, we are working to inform the world of all that I witnessed.

Your Excellency, I know that my activities have made me many enemies. I live every single day with the fear that they will kill me. Threatening emails from anonymous senders are piling up in my inbox. Most of them demand that I cease what I am doing. Occasionally they are filled with abuse, urging me to kill myself.

They have been surveilling me for a long time now. Last month I saw as clear as day that the driver from the Chinese food delivery service who came to my home had dark skin and bulging eyes. I disinfected the entire house and checked for wiretap devices. I contacted the restaurant to demand the identity of the delivery driver, but there was no response. Recently, when a virus notification popped up, I became certain that someone had hacked into my computer. I requested personal protection from the police, but, again, I didn't get any kind of response.

Demonic shadows flicker at my window. I hear someone tapping on the glass. A thick hand comes in through the window and tries to open the door by force. The skin on the hand is mottled with dark patches like a corpse and knobbled like a toad, the fingernails rotted black. Horror claws at my heart, and it's as though my blood is being drained to the last drop.

It must be that, as my life force dwindles, the hallucinations I suffer from are growing more severe. I'll have to increase the dosage of my medications. But until this life of mine dries up completely, I will not cease my fight against th . . .

Th . . . th . . .

Those eyes, those eyes . . . !!

Author's Note to the Korean Edition (May 2020)

After putting my stamp on the contract for this book, I kept agonizing over one question: "What exactly is Cthulhu and cosmic horror?" Now that it was actually coming time to write, I knew nothing. Reading through a Lovecraft story collection and books related to Cthulhu one after another, it felt like I knew even less. What is it that makes the feeling of "Cthulhuesque"?

At first, I imagined a huge monster. The first image of the book came out of that. But I soon knew that wasn't it. The moment I imagined that there was a physical substance and ways of standing up against it, that story wasn't Cthulhuesque at all. Talking it over with friends, the one conclusion I came to was that there has to be something omnipotent that has absolute malice, and the horror experienced by a powerless human who, faced with this, can know nothing and do nothing to resist. But powerlessness was never my style, so I came to racking my brains over what could be the means for becoming helpless even without being powerless. Anyway, I was thinking of putting in "The Call of Cthulhu." There we see the means for getting rid of Cthulhu.

What I was curious about while reading "The Shadow Over Innsmouth" was "Why on earth did the villagers pursue the protagonist?" It's not as if he could have been the only person to have ever stopped by the village. My imagination was also stoked by the thought that, aside from the chase itself, all of the horror occurred only in the protagonist's mind. And from there I became curious about how the villagers lived, and also with what kind of gaze they would have perceived the protagonist. I just hoped that writing the hidden side of a story wouldn't betray the feeling of the original. I hope I have not offended readers who like Cthulhu mythology.

With the onset of the COVID-19 era, it seems as though the story has become particularly timely, but of course the contagion in the story and COVID-19 infection have different conditions. And so it follows that the meaning of quarantine in the story is different too. I am grateful to all the medical staff who are fighting in this pandemic time, and deeply mourn those who have passed.

Looking into Lovecraft's life, they say that his father died of a sudden-onset mental illness when he was still a boy, and the sudden death of his maternal grandfather who had taken him in meant that family fortunes collapsed and he couldn't finish school, and his mother died in a mental institution not long afterward. It seems to me that, for someone who has lived through such a life, stories of there being an absolutely evil god out there somewhere and humans who are faced with it inevitably being powerlessly swept up in misfortune would be irresistibly captivating. I can see how imagining the existence of an evil god could have been a way to console his misfortune, which must have been impossible to understand or accept.

I am grateful to writer Lee Suhyeon for inviting me to join the Lovecraft Reanimated project, and being so generous with encouragement and help throughout the writing process. Thank you to Koh BumChul for all the in-depth debates on Cthulhu mythology, Alma publishers for bringing such a project to completion, and editor Yoo Seungjae for sticking it out with me.

Acknowledgments

TK

ABOUT THE AUTHOR

Author photo TK

Hyeyoung

Kim Bo-Young, one of the leading science fiction writers in Korea, began her writing career in 2004, winning the inaugural Science and Technology Creative Writing Awards with her novella *The Experience of Tactility*. Her first novel, *The Seven Executioners*, received the Grand Prize at the 1st Annual SF Awards of Korea, while her short story "How Alike Are We" won the Grand Prize in the short story and novella category at the 5th Annual SF Awards of Korea. In 2021, her short story collection *On the Origin of Species and Other Stories* was long-listed for the National Book Award for Translated Literature, and her short story "Whale Snows Down" was short-listed for the Science Fiction and Fantasy Rosetta Awards. Bo-Young's work has been translated into a number of languages and is read worldwide. Her writing has been praised by award-winning film director Bong Joon-ho. She was a script adviser for Bong's 2013 film *Snowpiercer*.